Pieces of Silver

A Starian Tale Novella

Iris Foxglove

Author's Note

Please be advised that the natural power exchange/biological imperative kink element to this story is intended as fantasy, **and should not be considered a factual representation of BDSM as practiced between consenting adults in real life**. The dynamics portrayed in this and other Iris Foxglove titles are entirely fictional, and should not be considered a guideline for the safe practice of any activity described herein.

CW for this story include: mentions of bullying, mild sexual harassment (not from any main character), references to misuse of power, very mild violence and graphic sexual situations. Please feel free to contact the authors for any further information if necessary.

This story was originally posted bi-monthly on Patreon for our House of Onyx tier members. The bonus story that follows the novella is also a Patreon exclusive. Content has been edited and formatted for publication. If you'd like exclusive content, monthly bonus stories, audio codes and sneak peeks of future projects, be sure to check out our Patreon!

formatted for publication. If you'd like exclusive content, monthly bonus stories, audio codes and sneak peeks of future projects, be sure to check out our Patreon!

Chapter One

Two weeks before Prince Adrien de Guillory was to be crowned king, the captain of his father's royal guard woke to the sound of someone drumming on his door.

"Please." Ferrin pushed the coverlet down and swung his legs over the side of the bed. "Let me have a moment's peace."

The person at the door kept knocking. Ferrin groaned. Peace was unlikely for anyone in de Guillory's employ. King Emile was a magnet for trouble, and his son was much the same. In the past ten years of service, Ferrin had faced over half a dozen attempts on the king's life, two disappearances, and a string of charges levied against the nobility by the prince himself. A son of a traitor was going to be the left hand of the future king. There was some sort of magical spirit following the king's lover around, and Prince Adrien saw the future in cups of water. It stood to reason that the weeks preceding Prince Adrien's coronation were going to be difficult.

"Let me guess," Ferrin said, slinging on the coat that hung from a hook by his bed. "There's a dragon loose in the palace. No. *Two* dragons and one of them talks, so we're going to befriend it and make it the Minister of State."

"Sir?" The person at the front door had finally stopped knocking. "Captain?"

"Or there's an assassin made of sentient knives," Ferrin muttered. He stepped into a clean pair of uniform trousers and picked up his belt from its place in a basket by the front door. "And Lord Harris has fallen in love with it."

"Um?" There was another, considerably more tentative knock. Ferrin grabbed the comb—which he'd left in the same basket as the belt—and ran it through his hair before he opened the door to reveal Private Jameson, one of the new recruits in the palace guard. "Sir. I was told you were needed on account of, um. The new recruits being signed in?"

Ferrin only just stopped himself from sighing. Right. They had a whole slew of newcomers to the guards now that Prince Adrien was being crowned. Most of them came from the common folk in the lower city, who seemed to view Adrien as a sort of folk hero, and their job for the first few weeks of their stay in the guard was to stand upright, look pretty, and not fall asleep while high-ranking officials made speeches about progress.

"Thank you, Jameson," Ferrin said. "I'll be right out once I've made myself presentable."

"You aren't already?" Jameson asked and pressed his lips together when Ferrin gave him a look. It was the same look employed by fathers the world over, the kind that could stop a misbehaving child in their tracks, and despite the fact that Ferrin had no children, he'd mastered the look two years into his tenure as captain. It worked remarkably well on the palace guard, and Jameson was no exception, guiltily stepping back with his cheeks flushing pink.

"I'll be out in a moment," Ferrin said and closed the door.

It didn't take long. Everything in Ferrin's small row house was in the same place it had been when he'd first moved in, down to the keys kept in a bowl by the door. The walls and floor were bare, but there didn't need to be much decoration, as Ferrin rarely kept visitors, and he mostly used the house as a place to sleep and store his uniforms. He had one book on the nightstand, given to him by an ex-lover who insisted he take up a hobby that didn't involve herding kings, but he'd only managed to get halfway through.

When he stepped into the street, his face freshly scrubbed and his sword hanging from his hip, Ferrin looked up to find that the sun was only just creeping up over the horizon. Duciel, the capital city of Staria, was shaped much like an overturned bowl, which meant that the shadows moved dramatically along the spiraling streets when the sun rose. The effect it had on the palace was dazzling. On a clear morning, it looked like the sun was rising twice—once over the horizon and once at the top of the hill, reflected off the polished walls and high glass windows of the palace.

The palace was already awake when Ferrin got there. The servants' entrance was busy with movement, lines of people sweeping in and out with deliveries and messages, people pulling each other up on hanging platforms to pin up banners and flags. Someone was even scrubbing the statue of the first king, which Ferrin thought was rather pointless, as the pigeons would just wait until they'd left to roost on it again. He passed them all by, followed by a wide-eyed Jameson, who was green enough to still find the palace awe-inspiring.

There was nothing awe-inspiring about the new recruits, at least, who were gathered together in a disorganized huddle in the barracks. Their uniforms were sharp enough, brand new tunics and sashes commissioned by the Master of the Royal Wardrobe, but half of them had left their sashes undone, and at least two had put their tunics on the wrong way around. They tried to move into straight lines when they saw Ferrin walk in, but there was a good amount of jostling and cursing, and Ferrin had to bite down a smile.

"Ah," he said, as over two dozen young people looked at him askance. "I see."

Then he turned on his heel and left.

He gave them five minutes to panic, then walked back in to find one of the tunics turned the right way, most of the guards standing at some form of attention, and every pair of eyes fixed his way. Good. That was better.

"There you are," he said. "Private Lamb, your tunic is on the wrong way around."

"Oh, no," whispered the guard. She frantically started trying to twist it back.

After going over roll and reminding them all that they were supposed to be guards, actually, not children playing pretend, Ferrin left them to their drills and checked in on the day shift, where most of his more seasoned guards were on duty. They all greeted him properly, with none of the slight panic of the new recruits, and Ferrin picked out five of his most trusted guards to see to the prince and make sure he didn't run off to Mislia or start a minor revolution in his spare time. When it came to the de Guillorys, one could never be too careful.

Ferrin, meanwhile, was to report directly to the king—King Emile, for now, though he was already well prepared for Adrien to take over. Half of Emile's things had been packed off and sent to a country estate, and when Ferrin arrived at his bedroom door, Emile appeared with his hair disheveled and his coat unbuttoned.

"Captain Ferrin," he said. "Do stay where you are, thank you."

He closed the door. This, Ferrin assumed, meant that the

king's lover was currently tied to the bed, or the balcony, or perhaps the tea table. It was always a toss-up with Emile. Ferrin waited by the door with the same straight posture and placid expression he'd mastered as a recruit, doing maths in his head for the cost of new swords while the king finished fucking his lover.

Emile appeared again twenty minutes later, having bathed in the interim, with flower blossoms stuck to his hair and a pleasant smile.

"Well, Captain," he said, buttoning only one of his shirt cuffs as Ferrin stepped out of attention. "How many death threats today?"

"None so far, your majesty, but the day is still young."

"Yes, let's see who we can manage to infuriate," Emile said. "Starting with you. I have work for you, Ferrin."

Ferrin didn't blink. Emile always had work for him. He was *King Emile,* one of the most controversial kings of the past century. The fact that his son was determined to take that title, too, just went to show they weren't quite as different as the gossip rags assumed.

Emile started off down the hall, still looking half dressed, while Ferrin kept at his side. Behind them, Ferrin's pick for the king's guard walked at a respectful distance.

"I don't know if you were around for my coronation, Captain," Emile said. "Were you? I believe another man was captain then, large fellow, an unfortunate beard..."

"Captain Withers, your majesty. You shot him, I recall."

"Oh, yes."

As though Emile would have forgotten. Withers had been furious at having his captaincy revoked, and Ferrin, who was only a sergeant at the time, had been the unfortunate one Withers had turned to when he needed a sympathetic ear. So when he'd learned that Withers was planning to "gut the bastard," as he put it, Ferrin had quietly brought the matter to the king.

Who had, quite calmly, waited until the next morning to take the ceremonial gun from Withers's hip, shoot Withers point blank, and hand the gun back to Ferrin.

"I think you should hold onto this, Captain," he'd said as the body collapsed on the rug. "Keep it out of the wrong hands."

Now, Emile was not the same man who had killed his former guard captain. He was less tense, more likely to flash a sardonic smile. It wasn't a sea change, but it was there and certainly noticeable to Ferrin. And since he'd declared his intentions to abdicate, he'd been practically *jovial*.

"Well, you'll be pleased to know you have a role to play in the main event," Emile said, passing the long row of windows that lined the hall to the council chambers. "It's terrible. You have to dress in a cape and hand my son a sword, and he has to cut off a lock of your hair." He glanced at Ferrin, whose dark hair was cut short, and shrugged. "Perhaps you'll have time to grow it out. But you'll need to speak with the Mistress of Ceremonies, Selene, and pop by the Master of the Royal Wardrobe for your cape."

"Yes, your majesty. I do have a cape with my formal uniform."

"Yes, but this one will have bells. Literal bells, Captain. I would say I'm sorry, but I'll be in fifty pounds of fur and silk, so I have no sympathy to spare."

"Sire," Ferrin said and bit his tongue as Emile turned.

"Is that a *Yes, sire* or a *Please don't do this, sire?*" Ferrin said nothing, and Emile smiled. "Yes, I knew you'd be thrilled. Go see to it now while I'm at council. I'll have de Valois there to take your place."

Ferrin wanted to remind him that a duke with a fondness for the blade wasn't the same as a guard, thank you, but instead, he simply bowed, keeping his expression carefully blank. Emile clearly got the message regardless, as he raised one brow and waved Ferrin off.

Emile wasn't exactly a difficult king to serve. Oh, he managed to make enemies simply by breathing, that much was true, but when people brought up his paranoia and dark moods, Ferrin had always shrugged it off. He knew he was loyal, and so did the king. If the king's opinion turned on him—as it had, it seemed, on other less fortunate people—then Ferrin at least knew how it would happen. Quick and clean, one shot in the heart, with the weapon hanging close at hand on Ferrin's hip.

He touched the handle of the gun as he headed down the stairs. It had one round loaded and was a devil to shoot—Emile must have been well-trained or exceedingly lucky when he killed the former captain. Ferrin had handled guns in the past, though the means of making them was such a carefully-guarded secret that even the navy had a limited supply. Anyone caught making their own was sentenced to a long life in a dark cell somewhere, and no one wanted to take that risk unless they were a pirate, as they were doomed anyway.

A cape with bells on was close, though. Hell. Ferrin sighed and turned toward the workroom kept by the Master of the Royal Wardrobe. Ferrin was the sort of man who preferred to tackle the most unpleasant tasks first, and being fitted for an outfit that made him look like a pompous jester was certainly the worst.

"Please let it not be velvet," he whispered and took a moment to compose himself again before smartly knocking on the workroom door.

* * *

The Captain was here.

"I'm fine," Silver breathed, staring at the pile of fabric, a pair of scissors, and a collection of leather thread on the table. There was no reason to be so worked up over what was really just another appointment, for a—a cloak, something with bells, that wasn't hard. He'd be able to get it done before lunch, probably. While he was dying quietly inside because there was something about Captain Ferrin that just made Silver absolutely *feral* every time he saw him.

It wasn't just how good-looking the captain was, either, though he was certainly that; tall, short dark hair and dark-eyed, with powerful shoulders and a neat beard. He had a deliciously deep voice with the slight cadence of the lower city in his clipped vowels. Sometimes Silver would imagine what it must be like to be one of the guards and think how he'd probably *die* the first time Ferrin corrected his posture or whatever—Silver wasn't actually sure what sort of things went into being a soldier. Or a guard, rather—wait. Were they the same?

To Silver, Master of the Royal Wardrobe, it didn't much matter if soldiers were guards or guards were soldiers. To the man he'd been before, well. Anyone with a sword and the authority to use it was a *problem,* no matter what they called themselves. Now, he knew what the various insignia on a guard's uniform meant, could recognize the difference between a royal naval officer and a sailor from the cut of a coat alone... and still wanted to faint every time Captain Leonhart so much as looked at him.

It wasn't just that he was handsome. It wasn't even the firm, heavy dominance that made Silver want to kneel every time Ferrin so much as glanced his way, though that was part of it. It was the fact Ferrin was so...imperturbable, so calm, so obviously, perfectly comfortable with himself and the life he lived. Nothing rattled him, not serving the *king*, not dealing with recruits, not—not that whole thing with the assassin who wore other people's faces. He was stalwart and brave and loyal, dependable, and Silver had any number of fantasies about him being all of those things while he made Silver kneel.

The knock came again. Silver startled, shook off his sudden panic, and went to fling the door open with a smile. "Oh, hi! Captain, ah. Captain Leonhart."

Captain Gorgeous Face Leonhart stared at him, impassive and impossibly tall. "Hello, Ser Crowe."

Silver laughed, which was not what he meant to do, but it was better than kneeling and asking Ferrin to let him kiss his— very shiny—boots. "Ah. Hi. You're, um, here for the fitting?"

"Apparently so, yes."

Silver smiled brightly, clinging to the door jam with his fingers like he might pitch over if he didn't.

"May I come in," Ferrin said, slowly, carefully. "Or are you intending to do this here in the hallway?"

Right. People had to come in for Silver to do the whole... tailoring thing. Silver moved back and felt the tips of his ears go red, but he busied himself with the measuring tape around his wrist and tried not to feel like an utter fool for how he inevitably acted like a drunk squirrel around the incredibly put-together Ferrin.

"I'm supposed to have some contraption with bells," Ferrin said, moving to stand by the mirror. Great, now there were three of him, so tall and hot. "The king insists."

Silver blinked. "Oh, right, the—cape, with them? He mentioned that."

"Yes." Ferrin watched him in the mirror and said in that beautiful voice full of natural dominance, "I don't mean to hurry you, Ser Crowe, but if you could...I do have a busy schedule with the coronation imminent."

Gods, he was so—that voice, that dominance—Silver felt the

urge to kneel and instead pulled at his hair, smiling again, too bright. "Sure. Sorry. So, are you excited?" He grabbed his measuring tape, the charcoal stick, and his notebook and went about taking measurements. He'd fitted Ferrin for a new coat for the prince's wedding, and still, touching those broad shoulders made his cock stir and his face flush.

"About the measurements?"

"No!" Silver laughed, only a little wildly. "The coronation."

"Oh. Yes, I suppose so. Mostly I will be glad when it's over." Ferrin stood still as a statue while Silver dragged a box over to stand on to finish the measurements of his impossibly broad shoulders. He wished he could just...touch Ferrin, rub those tense shoulders, relax him. Then blow him. Then lay on his face on the floor and let Ferrin fuck him into the hardwood. That'd be great.

"You'll miss His Majesty?" Silver asked, around a mouthful of pins. He did like to think that he was good at his job, and while he'd lied a few times about his experience, he enjoyed making clothes, and the job was far more suited to his nervous energy than his...last position.

"I'm glad for him if you want the truth," Ferrin said, meeting his eyes in the mirror. "I know he's got a reputation, but he's... he's not a bad man. I think he should go somewhere with his man, smell the flowers. Leave politics to his son, who is better at it."

Silver didn't care much for the politics of the court, but he knew King Emile wasn't the most-loved man in the kingdom. But he'd never been anything but helpful for Silver, really, even if it was designing his submissive's clothes that earned Silver his favor. King Emile was vaguely terrifying, but his dominance wasn't the kind that made Silver trip over his own feet, so he'd never been particularly bothered in the king's presence. He was much shyer around Prince Adrien's consort, for example, than the king. Emile de Guillory, with his perpetually messy hair and slight smirk, only had eyes for his submissive. And Silver was almost a thousand percent sure he wasn't the king's type, anyway.

"I like him," Silver said, noting the measurements even though, if he were honest, he already knew them. "The, ah. King's submissive. Bazyli? I've even seen him smile."

"Yes. I like him, too. You weren't here, were you, when the queen was alive? He loved her. When she died, well, it made him a different man. He's only just thawing out a bit, I think."

Silver smiled as he remembered the way the king stared at his submissive in the corseted vest Silver made for him. He'd made several more over the last two years. But he liked that Ferrin was sharing this sort of thing with him. Like he was *trustworthy*. Like he really was the royal tailor. Which he was, but that wasn't it. He also had a past, and at least now, he could be in the same room with Ferrin, and the only reason he couldn't breathe was from a mortifying and intense attraction, not the old fear that Ferrin would recognize him and toss him in the dungeon.

"It's hard to lose someone," said Silver, who'd lost exactly no one, but then again, he'd never really had anyone to lose. "But no, I wasn't here for that."

"You're too young, I'd imagine," Ferrin said. He studied Silver in the mirror. "Are you going to put me in velvet, then? The king said it'd be velvet."

The way his accent became just a little more pronounced when he spoke to Silver, oh, that did things to him, to hear that little burr that the captain didn't usually let show. He probably thought Silver was just another lower-city kid who made good by having luck and a talent for sewing, which was...sort of the truth.

"You're not the velvet sort, Captain," Silver said, reluctantly stepping off the box and away from the six-foot-whatever of beautiful man standing there. "You look great in red, but I think dark blue would be best, like a river. Maybe a hint of silk, something shimmery? You're like, ah. A stone underwater."

"Is that so? Worse things I could be, I suspect. And I don't hate blue."

"You shouldn't." Silver couldn't imagine there was a color on the planet that wouldn't look good on Ferrin. He looked amazing in the royal uniform's crimson, gold, and white, but the dark blue Silver had in mind for the cape—with gold bells woven in for the ceremony—would look wonderful on him. He had the reddish-brown skin common to those from Gerakia, and Silver was already imagining just how striking Ferrin would look in his polished boots and shining sword, dark blue silk swirling around him.

He was just about to—sadly—tell Captain Leonhart that he didn't need him any longer (unless he wanted to put Silver under, which would be *amazing*) when the door to his workshop was flung open, and Luca Miscali came flying through the door. Luca, a guard with aspirations of theater stardom, was one of Silver's most frequent visitors. They sometimes played dice and went to the pub together, but mostly it was because Luca needed something fixed on his uniform almost without fail every other week.

He was just about to ask *what size button* when he watched Luca snap a salute and face Captain Ferrin.

"Captain," Luca said, breathing hard, his eyes wider than Silver had ever seen. "Come quick! Someone stole the crown!"

"The—what," Ferrin snapped, going from easygoing to competent so fast, Silver shivered a little in his muddy, hastily tied boots. "The crown of *Staria*?"

"Yes," Luca said, faintly vibrating. "The—the *real* one," he said, which didn't make sense to Silver—they had fake crowns? —but it must have because Ferrin's dark eyes went wide, and he took a few steps toward the door.

"Tell me what happened," Ferrin snapped, and for some reason, Silver found himself following them toward the door.

He knew about a few things—tailoring, sewing, finding elements for people, that strange magic he'd inherited from his unknown parents back in his home in Diabolos. But before he was a tailor or the Master of the Royal Wardrobe, he'd been someone else.

Not Silver Crowe, but Crow...one of the most celebrated thieves in the Starian Thieves' Guild. And he'd left that life behind, but he couldn't deny the flash of interest at the thought that someone had really done it. Someone had stolen the crown two weeks before the coronation...and while he'd never turn in a former colleague, the curiosity was too much to ignore, and Silver just had to know how they'd done it.

* * *

Ferrin strode down the hall toward the throne room, boots clicking on the marble floor. One of the reasons Emile hadn't replaced him with a younger, less exhausted captain was because Ferrin didn't allow himself to make decisions in anger. Instead, he gathered the chaos around himself like a cloak and smothered it, giving himself the time and inner quiet to think.

A stone underwater, Silver had called him. He hadn't been so far off the mark.

"I want the guards posted at every entrance to note who comes out of the palace until further notice," Ferrin said as Luca struggled to keep up at his side. Silver was a steady presence at Ferrin's heels, keeping just a step behind him, but Ferrin didn't bother telling him to return to his chambers. For all that he chattered, Silver was not a gossip.

"Why do that when the thieves are already gone?" Silver faltered when Ferrin turned to look at him, and he blinked like a cat, slow and wide-eyed.

"Some thieves like to hide until the guards assume they've left."

"Oh." Silver's jolly tone sounded painfully forced. "Do they?"

Ferrin paused to look down at Silver, with his freckled face and sun-bleached hair and lay a hand on his shoulder. "You'll be quite safe here, I assure you."

Silver made a soft sound and nodded, and Ferrin continued down the hall.

For all that the palace was teeming with activity before the coronation, it was an organized chaos. After the troublesome business a few years back when an assassin took on the faces of other people—including Ferrin's, damn him—to get close to the king, Ferrin had instituted a new process for accepting outside assistance, vetting servants, and even allowing nobility to step into the palace. Nobles huffed and nattered on about it, but Ferrin's duty was to the crown, and a few disgruntled nobles and sighing servants were a small price to pay.

But it hadn't been enough, it seemed, because when Ferrin entered the throne room, Prince Adrien and King Emile stood at the open door behind the throne itself, staring into the empty room where the first crown of the Starian line was supposed to reside.

What Ferrin saw there when he entered was Sabre de Valois standing in front of an empty cushion on a plinth.

"Curious thing, isn't it?" Emile's voice had that dangerous quiet to it, the kind that used to set Ferrin's teeth on edge in the old days. "Here we have a room with a lock only one of the de

Guillory line can open, yet someone managed to take the crown from under our noses."

Ferrin nodded, looking up at Sabre. As the left hand of the future king, Sabre was in charge of the subterfuge necessary to keep Adrien alive, which clearly meant recovering missing crowns, as well. The first crown was supposedly the one that the first king of Staria wore, back when Staria was nothing more than a loose collection of villages and armies led by warrior kings. It was considered a symbol of power, used only during coronations and important affairs of state. Without the crown to give him legitimacy, Adrien's hold on the throne was tenuous. His enemies could use this against him, and the last thing Adrien needed was for the people of Staria to see an ill omen so soon before his coronation.

"I took the liberty of speaking to your guards at the doors," Sabre said as Ferrin examined the glass surrounding the velvet pillow. There were no marks from stray fingers, and the glass was unbroken. "There were five people in the throne room this morning. Myself—and you have full authority to search my rooms here or at the House of Onyx, if you so desire—a maid, Hana Lowering, who seemed to have gotten turned around and was escorted out, the Viscountess Fontaine, Lord Rousseau, and," he sighed, "a man with a green cloak who wouldn't give his name."

"Well, that certainly narrows it down," Emile said. "Why wouldn't your guards detain a man who wouldn't give his name, Captain?"

Ferrin bowed. "I will provide that answer shortly, I assure you."

"No need." Sabre lifted the glass gingerly to run a hand over the pillow. "I spoke with them. They said he was...very dominant and a bit forceful. They thought he was a noble by his speech. I sent word for my people to be on the lookout for a man of his description, of course."

His people meant spies. Ferrin wasn't sure how he felt about that. Lurking in shadows and whispering lies to one another to get an advantage was as far from Ferrin's preferred method as possible. Ferrin kept his notes precise. His guards knew exactly how to address him and provide information if needed, he knew their rotations and ranks, and everyone was as straightforward with one another as possible. It was the only way to prevent another man like Withers from trying to wrest control.

"What I don't understand..." Ferrin turned as Adrien approached the door, tapping the stone with his knuckles. "How did they even get in? The spell in the door responds to touch."

"Oh, I know that."

Ferrin winced as Silver appeared through the doorway, blushing pink as the most powerful nobles in the realm turned to look at him. The poor man really should have kept quiet. "I'll see him out, Sire."

"No." Emile raised a hand. "Silver, is it? Tell me, then, how do you open a door like this?"

Silver stood there a moment, mouth open, twisting his hands together.

"You can speak, lad." Ferrin felt for the man. He, too, had once been in his shoes—a commoner thrust into a position of power, all too aware that his life could end at the king's whim. "I can vouch for your whereabouts when the crown was stolen, after all."

Silver looked at him and nodded shakily. He didn't take his gaze off Ferrin when he spoke. "If I could, um, have one of his highness' gloves?"

"Why not?" Adrien smiled and peeled off his glove. Silver took it carefully and hovered at the door, holding it inside out.

"If you could let me close the door, please."

Sabre smiled, seemingly as bemused as Adrien, and he and Ferrin left the room. Silver closed the door, took a breath, and then slipped his hand into the inside-out glove. He touched the door again, and pale gold runes appeared along the frame before it popped open.

"I'm a tailor," Silver said. His voice sounded weak. "You wear something long enough, and an essence of you remains, right? So that's all a lock like this needs."

"I'm going to need all my locks redone," Emile said, and Silver hurriedly handed Adrien his glove. "Tell this to no one, Silver. I need not tell you the consequences should this information spread."

"Yes, your majesty. Of course. I, um, it's probably just that, well, there are spells like that all over Diabolos since there used to be a lot of witches there who magicked their things, so anyone from there would know. Sir. Your Majesty."

"Wonderful."

"Let me escort you to your rooms, Silver." Ferrin stepped forward before Silver could draw more attention to himself. Emile was in the beginnings of a nasty mood, and Silver was precisely the sort of person who could unwittingly set it off.

"Sorry," Silver whispered and flinched as Ferrin touched his back to guide him toward the door. Ferrin drew away—perhaps he didn't like being touched.

"You were very helpful," Ferrin said, "but this may get...complicated."

"Sounds like it already is." Silver tucked his hands in his pockets and hunched his shoulders. Ferrin only just stopped himself from correcting his posture. "You don't really think it's some guy in a cloak?"

"Not without evidence."

"Then it could be one of the others? The maid or the nobles?"

"It would be best not to speculate," Ferrin said, letting a note of warning slip into his tone. Silver nodded and hunched a little further. "Don't let this bother you. We have it well in hand."

He knew it was little comfort. When Ferrin was a boy living in the lower city of Duciel, he didn't take much stock in what a member of the guard had to say. Ferrin's family were law-abiding folk, but the guards who wandered Duciel during Queen Solange's reign didn't see the difference between Ferrin's family and the gangs of thieves who targeted wealthy folk in the market district.

When Ferrin announced that he was signing up to be a palace guard when he came of age, his parents had laughed. But the money was good, and King Emile let him do what he wanted with the guard so long as they didn't try to stab him in the back. A place in the palace guard was now one of the most coveted jobs for someone in the lower city, and while the city guard was out of his hands, Ferrin liked to think he had some sway.

Still, he knew it would take longer than his lifetime for any man in a uniform to be trusted by the common folk, and he had no illusions on the subject. Ferrin had a thief to deal with, and Silver was drawing too much of the king's eye as it was.

"Hey." Ferrin blinked, startled out of his thoughts. Silver was looking at him oddly, brows furrowed in concern. "Are you all right?"

"Ah. Yes, thank you." Ferrin gestured to the guard at the door to let them through and extended his arm. "Your help in this matter is appreciated."

"Oh, right. Okay." Silver hovered a moment, still looking up at Ferrin, and started toward the door. Then the door on the opposite end of the hall slammed open, and Silver jumped as

Ferrin turned to find two of his men carrying a struggling, cursing figure between the two of them.

"Sire," one called. Ferrin didn't like *that*. His guards answered to him first, then he provided their information to the king if it was necessary. He strode forward, and the guard saluted. It was Jean and Uriel, both senior guardsmen just a few years from retirement, leftover from Withers' tenure. Uriel nodded and saluted Ferrin, but Jean was too busy holding the man thrashing in his grip.

"Report," Ferrin snapped, and Uriel straightened to attention.

"Caught this man trying to sneak out with the cheese cart," Jean said and grabbed a fistful of the man's cloak. "Look, Captain."

Ferrin bit back a sigh. The man's cloak was green.

"Let go of me!" The man was young, perhaps still a teenager, with wild red hair and a pale face. "I didn't steal nothing!"

Uriel rolled his eyes and pulled a handful of pearls out of his pocket, and the man blanched.

"Don't know where those came from," he muttered. "I'm an honest man, I am, sir. You gotta believe me."

"Yes, he simply oozes the air of a law-abiding citizen," Emile said, and the man started to shake, staring from the king to Ferrin. Ferrin stopped and tipped up his chin to get a better look at him.

"The pearls aren't a good look, lad," Ferrin said. "What's your name? You can call me Captain."

"I'm innocent, Captain," the man said, and Jean grunted as he tried to drop to his knees. "Honest. I ain't never done nothing criminal in my life."

"We aren't discussing that at the moment." Ferrin let some of the dominance into his voice. "Your name, sir."

The man was breathing fast, hands flexing, and his gaze flickered throughout the room until it landed just over Ferrin's shoulder toward the opposite door.

"Armand," he said at last, in a small voice. "Armand Martin."

Chapter Two

O h, *no.*

Silver stared at the man he knew very well couldn't have stolen a crown and wondered if he was going to say something or not. He *should,* absolutely, because the king of Staria had a look on his face that suggested Armand was going to be a *guest of the crown,* and that would be bad. Thieves didn't hang or anything like that, but it was still difficult to afford the fees and bribes it would take to get someone out of hock. And Silver knew that Armand wasn't good enough at being a thief to get the guild behind releasing him. They'd make him do his time, pay his own fee, and he'd find the guild houses closed to him when he tried to go back.

Don't get caught was one of the most sacred rules of the guild, and Armand had broken it. Which meant he'd spend a few weeks or a month in jail, get out, be unable to pay his fees, and go right back to stealing to keep from being shipped off to the quarries or conscripted into the army. And Silver knew that for Armand, being in jail and unable to provide for his siblings would be the thing that sent him to more dangerous, risky jobs— the kind that *didn't* come with the guild's protection—and would likely end with him on a ship or his back breaking under the brutal labor of the quarries.

Armand should have never been given a spot in the guild, not when he tried to *steal from the palace*, which was bold and ridiculous and clearly out of his league.

Armand was not a good thief, but after a single glance at Silver, he didn't say anything else or try to use the knowledge of Silver's true identity to earn his freedom. Which was a rule, even if Silver—or Crow, as they called him—was no longer part of the guild. You didn't sell out former *or* current members, and Silver realized that also applied to him, too.

And even if it hadn't...Armand's siblings were both under twelve. They'd be alone if Armand went to jail, and Silver couldn't let that happen. He took a step forward, then glanced at the king and the prince, and finally at Ferrin. "Captain Leonhart, may I talk to you for a moment? Privately?"

Ferrin narrowed his dark eyes, but he nodded and jerked his head toward an alcove. "Jean, keep our—ah. Keep Armand here. Your Majesty, Your Highness. If you'll excuse me for a moment."

Silver tried his level best not to look at Armand, but he could feel the younger man's eyes on him as he followed Ferrin toward the alcove. He was frantically trying to think of what he could say and realized with a sinking feeling of dread that this could be the end of it; his new life, where he wasn't Crowe the thief, but *Silver* Crowe, Master Tailor of the Royal Wardrobe.

But he couldn't let Armand go to jail for something he hadn't done, could he? No. He remembered the little moppet of a girl who was Armand's youngest sibling, the way she'd looked at a day-old bread roll like it was a feast, and how she marveled at the steam from a hot bath that was all for her. The guild wouldn't throw them to the wolves, necessarily, but they had rules and regulations to keep everyone safe...and sometimes that didn't end well for the dependents of would-be thieves who hadn't yet proven themselves worthy enough to earn the guild's more *intensive* protection.

"Well?" Ferrin crossed his arms over his chest.

Silver took a deep breath. "It's not him. Couldn't be."

"How do you know? I've found thieves—even the boldest of them—could be anyone."

"Yeah." Silver closed his eyes. He could still stop this. Make something up. Hell, he could blame his magic if he wanted. *His elements are all wrong for priceless artifact theft.* But he knew he wouldn't do that. "It's just that the guild would never send him on this job, and no one but the guild would take it in the first place."

There was a heavy moment of silence, and then Ferrin said, in a very dangerous voice, "How exactly do you know that, Master of the Royal Wardrobe?"

Silver kept his eyes squeezed shut. "Because I wasn't always the Master of the Royal Wardrobe. I was someone else. Someone who would know that."

"You were a thief."

Silver opened his eyes. He felt—he wasn't sure there were even words for it. The look on Ferrin's face was mostly the same, but there was a slight suspicion in his narrowed eyes, and Silver felt, somehow, like he'd *disappointed* Ferrin. Which wasn't a good feeling, either for himself or that blasted biological urge to submit and please...which honestly, he'd wanted to do for Ferrin the second he saw him.

"I was," Silver said because there was no point in lying. "A good one. And even I wasn't good enough to do something like this. I'm not, now," he added quickly, pretending his heart wasn't sinking as he saw Ferrin's fingers brush the hilt of his sword. It wasn't as if he had a chance with the guard captain, even if all he'd ever been was a tailor. "And Armand. He's got little siblings. He wouldn't do this."

"He's a thief, you just said," Ferrin replied.

"I said the guild would never send him, and I meant it." Silver raked a hand through his hair, and he couldn't quite meet Ferrin's eyes. "I'm not a thief. I'm a tailor. But I have a past, yeah, and it means I know it's not him. Please, I—if you have to, um, arrest me or whatever, that's fine, but—" he swallowed, unsure what he was going to add there. But what? Don't fire him? He doubted he'd *hang*; this wasn't the lawless outer ring of islands near Diabolos. But relieve him of his position? That, Ferrin could do. And probably would, honestly. No one wanted a thief loose in the palace.

He was King Emile's favorite tailor, but King Emile wasn't going to be the king very much longer. And besides, ruining his son's coronation was probably not worth the few sexy outfits Silver created for Emile's submissive.

"I'm not going to arrest you. You haven't done anything." Ferrin straightened. "But you *are* going to come with me. I have questions, and you'll answer them, understand?"

The dominance in his voice made Silver shiver, and he was too keyed up to hide it. "Yeah. Of course. Just, uh. The pearls, if you want, I can handle those?"

"Are you asking me or telling me," Ferrin demanded coldly, and Silver shrank back a bit from the sharpness of his tone.

Ferrin had liked him before this. Maybe not in the way Silver thought about at night in his bed, but he'd smiled at Silver, treated him like a—like a law-abiding, useful citizen. An honest, working man in a palace full of nobles. Now he was looking at Silver with suspicion, a cool sort of distance in his gaze, and maybe Silver was just imagining things, but either way, what choice did he have? Ferrin might go from treating him with friendly camaraderie to chilly civility, but that was better than sending Armand to jail—or worse—for being in the wrong place at the worst time, with a handful of pilfered pearls that were probably not worth all that much, to begin with.

"Asking," Silver said. "I think. Uh. Sir? Captain."

Ferrin swore lightly under his breath. "All right." He strode out of the alcove like some kind of hot, purposeful—well, guard captain—and walked over to the king. "I have it on good authority that this man isn't responsible for the theft, Your Majesty."

"Is that so." Emile stared at him. "And that authority would be, who, exactly? The hyperactive tailor?"

"Um, yes?" Silver rocked back on his heels. "I asked him to get me the pearls for my—for, um. Um. Something for the —theater."

Emile cast his eyes heavenward. "I see."

"Your Majesty," Ferrin started, glancing at Silver. "I have a lead if you'd permit me to investigate."

"Yes, yes. That's Ferrin's very polite way of telling me to mind my own business," King Emile said to his son. He stared hard at poor Armand, who had his head bowed and was crying, visibly trembling. "And honestly, lad, if you're going to *steal* from the *royal palace,* perhaps do something a tad more inventive than *putting what you stole in your pocket.*"

"I'll just pay for them," Silver said quickly, stepping forward —only to stop as Ferrin clamped a hand on his shoulder. Tingles of electricity ran down his spine from the warm, hard grip of his fingers through the gloves, and damn, Silver was *really* hard up for it.

"I'll take care of this, and I'll find the crown. It's my job." Ferrin's voice was heavy, and between him and the king, the dominance was enough to make Silver half-hard and want to kneel more than he'd ever wanted anything in his life.

"I have a tailor who is trying to protect a thief—a very bad one, might I add, who is still *lying* about *being* one, and a missing *crown two weeks before the coronation*, Ferrin, I highly doubt that—"

"Emile," a voice said from the doorway, deep and lovely. "Your mother's submissive won't leave me alone."

Bazyli Drakos—Bazyli de Guillory, technically, since he'd married the king even if hardly anyone knew that, and Silver only did because he'd made Baz's wedding clothes—walked in, the bells on his waist and in his hair softly jangling. He was a beautiful man, striking with his dark hair, sharp cheekbones, and his lovely dark blue eyes that were sometimes pure white. He had flowers in his hair, and as he walked across the floor, his eyes on the king, Silver saw Emile's stern expression ease into something less thunderous.

"He's working on a sonnet for dear Adrien's ascension and wishes you to accompany him on the lyre, my hawk."

"What," Prince Adrien said and sighed. "Why? No."

Sabre de Valois snorted softly, and Adrien shot him a glare. "See how funny you think it is when he writes one for *you,* dear cousin."

"What is happening here?" Bazyli asked, glancing at all of them. He squinted at Armand. "You. I saw that man in the hallway earlier."

"How much earlier?" Ferrin demanded, removing his hand from Silver's shoulder.

Silver felt the loss of it like a limb and realized his hands were already behind his back. He moved them apart and caught Sabre de Valois staring at him. Silver smiled brightly, then glanced at Armand, who still hadn't raised his head.

Why *had* the guild sent him at all? He wasn't the sort who could pull off a sleight-of-hand robbery of pearls in the middle of the day in a palace where there was even more activity than usual.

"An hour. Maybe less. I was—ah. Going to visit the garden."

"Hide behind a pot?" Emile said at the same time.

"He wanted to ask me about my *childhood*," Bazyli said, glaring at the king. "Trying to find a rhyme for *mistreated son of the odious archmage.*"

"Your Majesty," Ferrin said, sounding very tired. "If you'll let me handle this."

"Well, I haven't a choice, have I?" Emile waved a hand, his attention clearly on his submissive. "Come along, Baz, let's go hide you from Jules and his attempts to reduce your traumatic childhood to meter and rhyme. Ferrin, report to me once you have something to tell me, which best be sooner rather than later." Emile nodded at Sabre, then swept the room with his cold, piercing blue gaze. "No one in this room says anything. That includes you, lad, unless you *really* want something to cry about."

"Father," the crown prince said, sighing. "There's no need to make him more afraid. Captain Ferrin said it wasn't him."

"But he did steal from the palace," Emile pointed out. "Which seems like a rather foolish thing to do in the middle of the day, but what do I know?"

"Take Armand somewhere comfortable and safe, Duke de Valois. I'll send a guard to let you know when it's safe to release him. He won't be harmed," Ferrin added, that dominance back in his voice.

It took a few minutes for everyone to clear out, but Adrien gave Silver a slightly distracted smile, and Sabre—who must have noticed that Silver was halfway to kneeling—gave him a speculative look before heading out with a hand on Armand's elbow.

"Silver," Ferrin said. "I think you understand why I'm going to have to ask you to come with me."

Silver nodded. "Yeah. But honestly...what you want to

know, I think you should come with *me*. But, uh, you should probably. Look less like a guard."

"Why?" Ferrin stepped closer, and the tension made Silver's hands migrate behind his back again.

"Well, uh. I know what you want to know, and I know where to take you, but they won't let you in if you look like you're gonna arrest everyone."

Ferrin sighed. "All right. But come with me, I don't—I'd prefer it if you didn't leave."

I don't trust you and want you to stay where I can see you, was what that meant. Silver smiled, grim and unhappy, but he gave an easy shrug and said, "Lead the way."

* * *

Of course, Ferrin couldn't have a normal day.

It was the de Guillorys, he suspected. They were cursed. Not a single event with a de Guillory involved was free from scandal or general chaos, and now Ferrin had to deal with a *thief* having infiltrated the royal palace in the guise of a tailor.

Ferrin glanced at Silver, who was walking a step behind Ferrin with the look of a dejected puppy, and sighed. Former thief, then. He doubted Silver would have gotten away with stealing from the palace for years, but the revelation that Silver used to spend his time with pickpockets like that boy Armand had shaken him more than he expected. Silver was dependable. He was skilled, useful, and had made himself as much a fixture in the palace as Ferrin. And now it had turned out to be...what? A ruse? A front?

"You really should change, though," Silver said and looked down when Ferrin turned his way.

"That's the plan," Ferrin said. "I have spares at home."

Silver stiffened as Ferrin placed a hand on his back, but

Ferrin would be damned if he let Silver go traipsing about unsupervised when he was clearly connected to this somehow.

But Silver was right, damn it all. Armand was not the thief—just a pickpocket in the wrong place at the wrong time. It all seemed a little too convenient, all the same. His guards mentioned a man in a green cloak, and lo and behold, there he was, pockets full of pearls.

"Seems a little easy, though." Silver seemed to find it impossible to remain silent, and Ferrin struggled to suppress the urge to order him quiet so he could think.

"Easy? Stealing a crown is easy?"

"No, I mean finding a thief. Don't you think? A crown goes missing, and some street kid with no parents and kid siblings gets picked up with a handful of pearls?"

"He's an orphan?" Ferrin wished he hadn't heard that.

"Well. Lots of kids are, sure." Silver looked away, shoulders hunching slightly. "But the point is he won't be missed. Nobody will care."

"His siblings will."

Silver looked up at Ferrin incredulously. "They're children. Nobody cares about homeless kids. They'll get picked up by minnow catchers or...oh, no, I'll have to find them. I don't think the guild will look for them."

"And what do you plan to do with them?"

Silver shrugged. "I don't know. Something. Anything. I don't have much space at home, but maybe they can...but no, I'm under suspicion, aren't I..."

It was a strange experience—there he was, captain of the guard, and a former thief was the one fretting over the living situation of a group of orphaned children. Ferrin's mother would be horrified.

"I can send one of the guard to find them," he said a little gruffly.

"Then they'll *really* disappear." Silver squinted in the light as they stepped out of the side door toward the carriage yards. Ferrin kept a hand on him as they passed the stables and gossiping hostlers and steered him down the spiraling road to his townhouse. Silver glanced around them as they walked, and Ferrin found himself following his gaze—first to a bird on a fence post, then a stained glass window, then a row of sunflowers. He couldn't seem to settle on anything, and he kept moving his hands, fiddling with his sleeve or twisting his buttons back and forth.

What he needed, Ferrin thought, was a patient dominant to give him something to focus *on*. If Ferrin had a submissive like Silver, he would have put him through his paces years ago. Perhaps a posture collar would do, or forearm restraints. Just to start, in any case. He had a suspicion that Silver would need particular attention.

Not that he had any place thinking that of a colleague—let alone one who turned out to be a member of organized crime. Ferrin remembered the havoc gangs of pickpockets used to wreak when his sister was starting her business—they'd sweep through and leave her scrambling to pick up the pieces, with half the day's work ruined. Thieves didn't care how poor their marks were or whether the person they stole from had a family to feed at home. Joining forces under a guild was just a way to keep thieves beholden to one district, not to instate actual rules of behavior or ethics.

"How long were you with this guild of yours?" Ferrin asked, taking out the key to his townhome. He headed up the steps, Silver at his back.

"Do you mean, am I still with them? I'm not. I left when I took this post, actually. I know you don't believe me," Silver added, looking at his feet.

"I do." Silver gave Ferrin such a woebegone look that Ferrin almost asked if he really *was* an abandoned puppy in a former life. "That nonsense back at the palace about asking the boy to find you pearls? That was a lie and a poor one. This, I believe. For a thief—a former thief—you do wear your emotions on your sleeve. Take your shoes off when you come inside."

Silver obeyed immediately, slipping out of his boots as soon as he crossed the threshold. He looked around, wide-eyed, as Ferrin took off his own boots. "Do you live here, or is this another guard house?"

Ferrin frowned. "This is my home."

"Oh. It's very...very clean."

"My sister calls it a depressing excuse for a house, but to each their own." Silver almost smiled again at that but turned his face away at the last second. He hovered by the foyer, and Ferrin gestured to one of the chairs by the dining table. "Sit. Or stand, if that settles you. I'll be a moment."

"Settles me?" Silver blinked at him. If Ferrin didn't know for a fact that he was a terrible liar, he would have called him a passable actor because with his lips parted just so and a blush spreading across his cheeks, he looked precisely like the sort of submissive who lined the streets of the pleasure district.

"Don't tell me this is what you look like settled."

Silver's eyes widened as realization dawned. "Oh. No. Actually, when I'm under, I get all floaty, sort of, and ask permission for everything. And I tend to get really into riding people then but, I mean, that's not—that's not what we're, um, talking about."

Ferrin banished the sudden image of a dreamy-eyed Silver riding his cock. "Quite. Sit down and stay *put* until I—" He stopped as Silver promptly sat on the floor. "That isn't...well, they were my exact words. Stay there, then."

"Oh my gods," Silver whispered and put his head in his hands.

Ferrin made for his bedroom, half expecting Silver to bolt as soon as his back was turned. But when he checked, Silver was still sitting there, right in the middle of the floor.

If they weren't in the throes of a political disaster, Ferrin might have to give that a moment's thought. As it was, he had places to go, and apparently, looking like a guard was right out.

He stared at his closet, frowning.

"I have a tunic and...my uniform trousers shouldn't draw attention."

"You don't have anything that isn't a uniform?" Silver called from the living room.

"Not precisely."

Silver groaned. "Can I get up and see?"

"Very well."

Silver got to his feet and walked cat-quiet across the house into Ferrin's bedroom. Ferrin watched him scan the room before he settled on the closet, where he clicked his tongue at what he found inside.

"Oh, wait, there are these," he said, holding up a pair of trousers Ferrin's mother had given him two years ago. He opened a box in the bottom of the closet and pulled out—oh hell, the sweater his great-aunt had made him, with the black stripes going down the middle. "Huh. Yeah, you'll look less like a guard, at least."

"I'll look like a professor from Gerakia," Ferrin muttered and stripped off his uniform shirt. Silver let out a little gasp of breath and went still as Ferrin took the sweater from him. "My grandfather was from there, and all he wore were sweaters."

"Well. Um. You definitely don't look like a grandfather in that," Silver said in a squeak. Ferrin sighed when he saw the trouble—the sweater must have shrunk, or his great-aunt must have gotten the measurements wrong because it practically strained at the shoulders. Still, it would have to do.

He put on the trousers, which were a drab brown and clung a little too close to his thighs, and turned to Silver. "How do I look?"

Silver gaped at him for a moment. Ferrin expected him to rattle off his aesthetic or elemental signature or whatever else Silver used to determine what made someone fashionable, but all Silver managed was a very small, very weak, "Fine."

Fine would work. "Good. Then let's go."

"Yes, all right." Ferrin wasn't sure he liked this meek version of Silver. Being submissive didn't mean not having a spine, after all. But he supposed Silver was deflated after having been caught out. It was difficult to reconcile the Silver Ferrin knew with the thief he used to be. Ferrin opened the door first, and Silver shied away from him, drawing in closer to himself when Ferrin raised his brows.

"I will look less like a guard, I think, if you look less like a prisoner."

Silver blinked at him. "I'm not one?"

Ferrin stopped at the doorway. "I see no bars. You are simply a person of interest."

"Wonderful."

This time, when Ferrin cocked his head and raised his brows, Silver didn't cringe. "Lead on, then. Where precisely are you taking me?"

Silver hurried down the steps, hands in his pockets. He was always doing something with his hands, it seemed, unable to keep still for more than a moment. "The Greenfield Bakery."

"Greenfield?" Ferrin laughed. "You're saying Greenfield, the one run by Annabel Pepper, is a den of crime? We lived down the street from her as children."

"It's not a den, it's a spare room, and her name isn't really Annabel." Silver actually smiled again, and it transformed his face, temporarily bringing back the man Ferrin knew. "I was one of her delivery boys when I first came here."

Ferrin thought of the young people he often saw running through the streets of Duciel with baskets of bread in their arms and went cold at what Silver was implying. "Some of her deliveries are made by children."

"They're not all part of it," Silver said too quickly. "And she'll deny it. If you order a raid, her back room will be full of baking trays and flour. I'm just saying... being able to deliver to a dozen houses in a day'll get you noticed."

"Did you want to get noticed?"

Silver looked away. "I don't know. There was a thrill to it, you know? And the guild becomes a family, sort of, which helps when you don't really have one. You can get by, and back when I was a part of it, it was better than sinking into debt or trying to become a courtesan. Or a whore," he added, "in one of the brothels that aren't in the pleasure district. I know his highness is working on that, but it wasn't that long ago that no one cared."

Ferrin opened his mouth to protest, then shut it again. His own family had been poor as mice, but they'd managed well enough. His sister ran a bookstore in a nice part of town, he made enough to set up his parents in a row home overlooking the gardens, and his little brother was off touring in the navy. But he had a family with aunts, uncles, and cousins to help bail each other out when money was tight. For boys like Armand— like the young man Silver had been—they had no other choice.

The Greenfield Bakery was in the nicest part of the market district, just a few blocks from his sister's bookshop. Ferrin half expected to see Louise out for a walk as they passed her quiet little store, but she was likely still inside, and Ferrin didn't want to explain himself if she saw him with Silver. His family was constantly urging him to retire and settle down, and Silver was exactly the sort of man they would fall over in half a minute.

"What are you looking at?" Silver asked, and Ferrin picked up the pace. "Anyway, the bakery's..." Silver's face fell. "Armand's sister and brother are there."

Ferrin slowed as they approached the open door of the Greenfield. There were two children sitting on the bench outside, holding empty baskets and whispering to each other. They were dressed in ragged breeches and tunics that were too big for their skinny frames, and when they saw Silver, the youngest, who had long, lanky black hair and Armand's worried face, got up and raced over.

"Crow!" She hugged Silver around the middle, and Silver blinked rapidly before awkwardly patting her on the back. "It's been forever. I lost a tooth! Look, look right here."

"Armand's been gone all day." The older child, who couldn't have been more than ten, hunched over his basket. "He said it'd be an hour."

"Oh." Silver looked pained, but his expression shifted into tense good cheer. "I'm sure he'll be back soon enough, Phillip. Just wait here with Violette, yeah? I'll come out in a minute with a meat bun for both of you."

"Yes, but did you see my tooth?" Violette bared her teeth at him, and Silver nodded.

"Very neat, Vi."

"Yeah, I tied a string around it, and Phillip tied the string to a door, and then I cried, and Armand took it out instead."

"Who's your friend?" Phillip eyed Ferrin with the deep-seated suspicion of all urchins faced with a guard.

"Just my...man," Silver said, and Ferrin shot him a look. "My man, um, um, Jean. Jean Smithe."

Oh no, he really was a terrible liar. Ferrin nodded woodenly. "Nice to meet you, Phillip."

"Yeah, okay."

"Well! Time to introduce him to Annabel," Silver said, grabbing Ferrin by the hand. He towed him off, and Ferrin just caught a glimpse of Violette heading back over to the bench as they stepped into the warmth of the bakery.

Greenfield was a charming place, one that Ferrin went to more than once when he didn't want to bother cooking for the evening. There were meat buns on the counter, pasties, turnovers, steamed buns, and strings of candied fruit. Annabel was at the counter, plump and smiling, with yellow hair twisted in a fashionable spiral at the back of her head. When she saw Silver, she set down the tray of spiced cookies and bustled around the counter.

"My crow!" She wrapped Silver in a crushing embrace, and Ferrin stepped aside so as not to invite one of his own. As a baker, Annabel's arms were solid with muscle, and she didn't seem to know her own strength. Silver squeaked and grimaced as she lifted him off his feet. "Darling, you haven't been back in ages. And you brought a fellow with you. You're in need of sweet buns, I expect. With caramelized walnuts, I remember."

"Um, not here for...I mean, I won't say no," Silver said as Annabel plopped a pastry in his hands. She squinted at Ferrin.

"I know you from somewhere," she said. Ferrin tensed. "Yes. You're...oh. Your sister doesn't run the bookshop, does she? Louise?"

"I can't say," Ferrin said quickly and tried to avoid Silver's searching gaze.

"If you were, that would make you the disreputable brother." She turned to pick up a pastry stuffed with strawberries and handed it to him. "The one who won't find a man."

Ferrin sighed. Of course, that was what Louise would say.

"Except it seems you did find one. Well done, Crow."

Silver blushed, still holding the pastry in both hands like it was about to explode. "Annabel, this is about a delivery. A lost one."

Annabel's smile faded, and she glanced at the window, where Phillip and Violette were huddled together. "I see. Head to the back, dear, and I'll join you."

Silver handed his pastry to Ferrin and started digging in his pocket. "And give a meat bun each to the kids, maybe?"

Annabel took the coin and patted Silver's cheek. "See, this is why I knew you wouldn't be my delivery boy forever. You're too free with your coin, my crow."

Silver looked down, ears pink, and gestured Ferrin to a door behind the counter. Ferrin handed him his pastry back, and Silver took a bite as they headed toward the door.

"Same Annabel," he muttered. "Probably didn't even notice the kids were hungry, but she gave us pastries for free."

Ferrin looked Silver over as they passed rows of baking shelves, ovens, and wide counters where bakery assistants kneaded bread and twisted dough into knots. "Perhaps she was right, though—that you weren't meant for this life. The one you had."

"Doesn't erase the fact that it happened," Silver said. "This was my family for a while. I made bread right over there," he added, jerking his head to a table where a young woman was kneading enormous lumps of dough. Ferrin tried to imagine a young Silver there, fresh from a robbery, punching dough under Annabel's watchful eye.

"Do you think they're a family to Armand?" Ferrin asked. "If they won't even feed his siblings?"

Silver made a face, and he turned as Annabel came through the side door. Her expression was grim, and when she approached them, she gestured Silver and Ferrin to a rack of buns rising next to the oven.

"You understand," she said, eyeing Ferrin, "that discussing my poor delivery boy Armand has no bearing on my business? I run a respectable establishment here."

Ferrin nodded. He knew they couldn't control all crime in the city—that there was a crime lord near his sister's shop was alarming, but he couldn't risk putting Annabel's guard up when the crown was at stake. "Of course. You aren't responsible for what your delivery boy does on his time off."

Annabel flashed him a warm smile. "See, this is why people like you. The city guard would be stomping about, demanding payment to look the other way—unless we're pretending you *aren't* Captain Leonhart, who used to live a few blocks down when we were children? Not that you'd remember me, of course, but your family was so...respectable."

Silver sighed. "Annabel, Ferrin. Ferrin, Annabel."

Annabel smiled and took Ferrin's hand a second time. "I can assume Armand has been taken by the authorities," she said. "Since his siblings are drifting about like lost ghosts. And it happened in the palace if Crow is here."

"That's..that's right," Silver said. "They say someone stole something else from the palace. Something Armand didn't take. Something big."

"Like what?" Annabel asked. Silver didn't answer. "You don't think I can't be discreet, little crow?"

"I'm sorry." Silver twisted his hands behind his back, and Ferrin stepped closer to put a hand on his shoulder, steadying him. "It'll be bad if it gets out."

"But you think it might be a guild job?" Annabel sighed. "I wouldn't have accepted a commission at the palace. You know the rule, Silver. We don't entangle ourselves in the nobility in this part of town." She glanced at Ferrin and smiled. "Whatever business we run."

"So you think Armand acted alone?" Ferrin watched her carefully, looking for the lie, and Annabel met his gaze.

"None of us have taken a job at the palace. I would have known. But if Armand acted on another's orders, which is likely given that the boy has no decent thoughts of his own and is implicated, Silver knows what that means."

Silver looked up. "You gave me a chance when I was caught once."

Annabel patted Silver's arm. "You were caught by a city guard, not the king. He's lost his second chance already. Armand is a risk. He is on his own now. When—if—he comes back, we are not to speak to him. My people will not speak to his siblings, and our doors are closed to them. It's the same rule we've always obeyed, Silver, from the beginning. No excuses, no exceptions."

"You can't." Silver stepped forward, shaking off Ferrin's hand. "He's just a kid."

"So were you," Annabel said, and Silver clamped his mouth shut. "And you knew better than to go to the palace. You did good, telling me." Annabel stepped closer to touch Silver's cheek and turned to look at Ferrin. All traces of the smiling, bouncy woman upstairs were gone. "And know I had no hand in this, Captain. A single one of my people is touched, and you will learn how far my reach goes."

Ferrin thought of his sister, safely working in her bookshop just down the street, and nodded. "And if I see one of your people in the palace..."

"Fair enough." Annabel's smile was sharp. "An impasse, then. We won't touch the palace, and you won't touch us. What a gift you've given us, little crow."

"That isn't..." Silver's eyes were bright. "That's not what I came here for."

"It's what you have," Annabel said. "Go on, boy. I have baking to do."

Ferrin took Silver by the shoulder and was surprised to find Silver was trembling—but not, he suspected, with fear. There were angry tears in his eyes, and his brows were pinched, his jaw clenched tight. Ferrin led him out the back door quickly before Annabel could change her mind and want to tie up any loose ends.

"I'm sorry," Silver whispered as they emerged into the clean-swept alley behind the bakery. "I'm...I'm so sorry. I didn't think, I..."

"Silver." Ferrin placed both hands on Silver's shoulders, putting as much dominance into his voice as he could reasonably allow. Silver looked up at him. "You had good intentions."

"She practically threatened you just now."

"I've been threatened before." Ferrin backed Silver up against the wall, giving him something to lean against. He lowered his voice, even though there wasn't anyone around them to hear. "Think of what we've learned from this, Silver. She said she didn't know anything about a job in the palace. Do you believe her?"

Silver shook his head. "I don't know. I thought I would, but Annabel wouldn't let on if she did."

"The fact that she kicked Armand out of the guild so quickly means she might be cutting ties just in case. She might know."

"But she won't let me close enough to figure it out," Silver said.

Ferrin brushed a tear off Silver's cheek. "Maybe not. But there are others. And we can always ask Armand. Now. Keep your chin up, Silver. If I buckled after every setback, I'd never have made it to the palace. And neither would you, I suspect."

Silver smiled, a little weakly, and Ferrin released him. "Yeah. Yeah, I guess not."

"Then let's go." Ferrin nodded toward the street beyond the bakery. "There's still work to do."

Chapter Three

Of all the things Silver expected Ferrin Leonhart to do, bringing Violette and Philip home was not anywhere on the list.

Silver didn't think Ferrin would *arrest* them or anything, but he certainly didn't expect that Ferrin would simply collect them like a tired mama cat herding her kittens into a box. But that was exactly what he did, with the sort of implacable dominance that the kids didn't notice, but Silver absolutely did.

"You live in this whole house by *yourself?*" Violette asked, wide-eyed.

Philip elbowed her. "Be quiet, or he's gonna make us go to the *basement.*" He stared hard at his sister, then gave Ferrin a suspicious look and didn't even bother to lower his voice. "And there's probably monsters or something down there. Vampires. *Creatures* that he wants us to take care of."

"There aren't any creatures, and I don't have a basement," Ferrin said. "But I do have a balcony, upstairs off the bedroom, and sometimes a cat sleeps there. Maybe she's there now." His expression remained as impassive as ever, but there was a hint of a smile in his voice.

The kids went charging up the stairs, and Silver finally let out a slow breath. "Thanks," he said quietly. "For, uh. Being nice about this." It fell flat, and it wasn't quite what he meant or even wanted to say, but he had to say *something*.

"Being nice about what? Not ignoring the plight of children who don't have a home? I'm not heartless." Ferrin squinted at him. "We're going to have a talk, you realize. And I'll...have to tell His Majesty about this."

And then Silver could kiss his job goodbye. King Emile was a paranoid man. He'd already made that clear enough back when he'd first hired Silver as the master of the royal wardrobe. He wouldn't want to have a man who used to be a thief in the palace, much less around his son, who would take the throne in a few weeks.

"Yeah. Could you please tell him that I really didn't mean to lie? I just...took an opportunity." Silver was horrified to feel his eyes go hot, and he couldn't meet Ferrin's calm, dark gaze. "I did really like the job. More than, ah. My last one."

"What?" Ferrin was quiet, and then Silver felt a hand fall gently on his shoulder. "No. Look at me."

Silver dragged his gaze up to meet Ferrin's, and his whole body went hot. His need for submission was out of control, and feeling so unsettled was only making it worse. He should have done something about it long before now—but how was he supposed to know that he'd end up embroiled in a heist? Even tangentially?

"I meant the king will need to know about Armand and the children. Not—what you used to do. If anyone should understand being someone different than you used to be, it should be the king."

Silver gave a harsh laugh. "Why does that sound like maybe it's only true if you *are* a king?"

"Maybe so. But how's this—you help me find the crown, and

no one needs to know you used to have a history as a...person with a different profession."

"I was a thief," Silver said. "A good one, too. And I didn't want to do it anymore. I still don't."

"I know you to be a good tailor and a kind man," Ferrin said, and Silver's face *burned*. "But I have to say, I've never seen you stand still enough to be a thief. I'd assume you'd have to do that. Or be, ah." He coughed.

"Quiet?" Silver flashed him a grin, and even though he knew he shouldn't, he ducked away from the hand on his arm and bumped against Ferrin, neatly sliding his fingers into Ferrin's pocket. He held up his prize and dangled it from his fingers. "You don't have to be quiet, Captain," he said, laughing as Ferrin blinked and then grabbed for the watch he was holding. "Just distracting. To do the kind of thieving I did, anyway."

"I'll have that back, now," Ferrin said, eyes narrowed, but he didn't really seem that mad. "My father gave it to me when I joined His Majesty's guard."

Silver, possessed of some wild, completely inappropriate death wish, leaped backward and said, "Crows aren't just clever, they can *fly*—"

It happened so fast, Silver only saw him come near and then felt his fingers close like a shackle around his wrist, and then the world went spinny, and his heart started racing. Ferrin's fingers were warm, and he smelled so good....

And then Silver was blinking at a smirking, obviously amused guard captain, who'd pinned him against the far wall. "Not fast enough." He gently untangled the watch chain from around Silver's fingers and slipped it into his pocket, but he didn't let Silver go.

Silver couldn't seem to find his breath. He wasn't fighting or trying to get away because Silver wasn't a thief anymore, but he was *also* not a fool, and when a hot dom had him pinned by one wrist? Yeah. No watch in the world was worth it.

Ferrin's dark eyes were sharp on his, and Silver realized he was staring up at him, trapped and breathing too fast.

"You're no thief, Silver Crowe," Ferrin said, in a voice so full of natural dominance, Silver nearly melted into a puddle of frustrated, desperate submissive right there. "But you're not as fast as you think you are."

Silver could think of absolutely nothing to say, merely swallowed dryly and croaked, "Guess not." He recovered enough bravado after a moment to add, "But I would have just stolen it. Not, uh. Shown off like that." He wriggled cautiously and wondered if Ferrin would let him go.

"That what you were doing? Showing off?" Ferrin didn't let him go. Instead, he seemed to press a little tighter on his wrists, which...huh. That was the, what did you call it? Right. The opposite of letting go.

"Yeah," Silver whispered, and he wondered what was happening here. Besides the sudden and surprising real-life fantasy, because it couldn't be that easy. This was Silver, worried and desperately in need of submission, and Ferrin, who probably just wanted some sense of control.

Silver exhaled shakily, and when Ferrin murmured, "Look down, be good," he nearly moaned. Silver cast his eyes down, and he *did* gasp out loud when he felt Ferrin's fingers glance over his neck.

"And don't touch my things without asking," Ferrin said, and Silver was too turned on to notice the thread of humor beneath the natural dominance because he could laugh *anytime*.

"I—sorry," Silver managed and then felt Ferrin tip his chin with those warm, strong fingers.

"You're not," Ferrin murmured, leaning down. "But you want to be. Don't you? Want me to make you sorry?"

"Fuck, yes," Silver managed, and he shivered as Ferrin leaned down to kiss him—

—and then he heard footsteps on the stairs, and a voice call out, "Sir Guard Man Sir, I found the cat like you said and we want to *keep* it, can we, can we? It don't got a tag!"

Ferrin stepped back just as Violette came in, clutching a wriggling, small tortoiseshell cat. Silver, wild-eyed and breathing fast and achingly hard, wanted to tear at his hair in frustration. The little girl was too enamored of the cat to notice what had been going on, but Silver swore softly under his breath as his shaky knees barely kept him upright.

Fuck, he was hard up.

"If you are sure the cat doesn't have a home," Ferrin said as if he hadn't just been pinning Silver to the wall and sexily threatening to *make him sorry*.

"I'm pretty sure 'cause she's not got a collar," Violette said, which honestly meant very little—people had garden cats that came and went from people's houses all the time. "I'm gonna name her *Cuddles 'cause* she's so *cuddly*."

Right then, the cat meowed, hissed, and wriggled in the little girl's arms. She beamed and hugged the poor thing harder in response.

"How about you take care of—Cuddles, here—until someone looks for her?" Ferrin suggested.

"Nuh-uh," Violette said, eyes narrowed. "'Cause if they wanted Cuddles, they shoulda named her and given her a nice house like this one. Where's Armie?"

"He should be here soon," Silver said, trying for a normal voice.

"Why's Crow squeaking?"

"He's fine," Ferrin said quickly. "Would you like some food for Cuddles?"

Cuddles hissed when Violette put her down, but she seemed to come around to them when Ferrin gave her fresh water and some bits of sliced, salted fish from a tin. They made Silver wrinkle his nose—he didn't like seafood—but Cuddles seemed appeased and ate while occasionally giving them judgmental glances from her wide, yellow eyes.

"I'll need to find someplace for them to stay." Silver had finally recovered some of his equilibrium, and as he watched the kids play with Cuddles, the—mostly—quiescent cat, he started to think with his brain instead of his dick and his raging need to kneel for someone.

"I'd say they could stay here, but..." Ferrin glanced at the kids, who were batting a ball of crumpled paper for Cuddles to chase across the floor, and kept his voice low. "I don't know if their brother would want them all staying in the house that belongs to the king's Guard Captain."

Silver firmly told his libido to get it together and focused on the task at hand. "Probably not. And the guild might...get the wrong idea."

"The guild that threw him and his family out, you mean?"

Silver winced. "I know how it sounded, but there are rules for a reason. Armand hasn't...he would have been warned before. It's everyone who—what?"

"They are children," Ferrin said. "They've done nothing to deserve being thrown out."

Silver gave a brittle smile. "Yeah. You know, it's funny how that matters *now*, not when they were so desperate their big brother had to make a deal with the thieves guild in the first place! You know it's not just so easy for everyone here, don't you?"

"You know *you* walked into the palace and became the royal tailor, don't you?"

"Okay, fine, that's true enough. But I wouldn't have unless I knew how to sew." Silver waved a hand. "But they'll need to stay somewhere, and their brother will need to be with them. I have some money. I could maybe get them all a room for a few nights."

"That might give them a place for the night, but that's not going to fix the problem." Ferrin straightened. "They need something permanent. Which means he'll need a job. I think I have an idea."

"You don't, uh, want him to be a guard, right? Or the kids?"

Ferrin stared at him. "No. But my sister could use the help at the store, and she has rooms above that she rents out. The family who lived there just moved to the country, so they're empty. You stay here with the kids, and I'll go and talk to her."

"Wait," Silver said quickly. "While I'm, uh, flattered you trust me to stay here without stealing from you—" not that there was much here to *steal*, "—I think it's best if I go, too. The kids know me, yeah? They trust me. And I can explain about Armand to your sister."

Ferrin ran a hand through his short hair and sighed. "All right. But before that, I, ah." He cleared his throat, losing that bit of a burr in his voice and going back to proper guard captain guy again. "I should apologize for earlier."

Silver's heart sank, but he plastered a bright smile on his face and shrugged. "Don't. I get it. It's, ah. Been a day." But he didn't think he could hear Ferrin say it was a mistake, even though, yeah, it probably was.

"It has, yes. But it's not honorable of me to try and take advantage of a pretty submissive just because I feel like the last thing I had control of, today, was putting on my belt this morning."

Silver gave a strangled half-laugh. "Y—yeah." Great, now he was thinking about how Ferrin called him *pretty* and mentioned his belt in the same sentence. Silver wasn't one for pain, but he'd like it if Ferrin put that belt around his wrists or his neck. Or, oh, gods, in his *mouth*—

"And it was fairly impressive," Ferrin continued as if Silver wasn't dying right there in his living room. "What you did with my watch."

"I'm good with my hands," Silver said, unable to help himself. The look he got in return made his blood go hot. "Goes along with the job. Of being a tailor," he added weakly.

"And being honorable goes along with mine," Ferrin said, and then the ridiculous man *half-bowed* to him, Silver Crow, a man who made up every name he'd ever had and lied to become a tailor and now had a cat climbing up his leg to escape two very determined children.

"And now," Ferrin said, as if this were in any way normal, "Let's go to the Sanctum. My sister's bookstore."

"Can we bring the kitty?" Violette asked, hauling an unimpressed Cuddles into her arms and hugging her.

The cat meowed, and Violette hugged her harder.

"I suppose we can," said Ferrin and headed toward the door.

* * *

"Who *are* you?"

Ferrin stood outside his younger sister's bookshop with a drowsy kitten in his sweater pocket, two children debating how to split a skewer of fried dough, and the royal tailor he almost dommed in his own living room.

"Evening, Louise."

Louise grinned. She was dressed in her usual trousers and fitted blouse, and gold clasps glittered in her locs as she tilted her head to take Ferrin in. Her face, so like their father's with his arched nose and expressive brows, had the same look she'd worn when Ferrin was eleven and tried to bring a puppy home off the street. After decades of living in the same house and looking after their younger sibling, Wes, they'd developed a private way of speaking through facial expression alone.

"So," Louise said. "Been some time, Ferrin." She raised an eyebrow and glanced at the kitten, which meant, *who are you, and what have you done with my brother?*

"Thought I'd come and see how you're doing at the shop," Ferrin said, scratching his temple in a way that said, *you won't like this.*

Louise looked at the children, and her mouth twisted in a wry smile. *I'm not fooled.* "Come in, then. All of you. Yes, even the kitten. I was about to close up shop for the night."

"I know this place," Philip said, hanging back. "You're the witch lady who curses people what steals your books."

Louise beamed. "You've heard of me! Wonderful, I was hoping that rumor would pick up—I was having awful luck with this blasted fox that kept eating the books off my discount rack." She gestured to a hand-drawn picture of a boy with black eyes and a fox labeled "Banned for Book-Eating/Enabling."

"So you're not really a witch?"

Louise winked at Philip. "Who knows? Why don't you and your sister...can I have your names?"

"Philip, and I'm Violette. This is Cuddles." Violette held up the kitten for examination, and Louise smiled.

"I'm Louise Leonhart. You and your brother are both allowed to pick out one book for free."

"Can't read," Philip said, but Violette stared longingly at the books, holding the cat to her chest.

"Then pick one with interesting illustrations. You'll find

them over there. The adults and I are going to have a long, *long* talk." The look she gave Ferrin clearly said, *You're fucked, kiddo.*

"Oh, boy," Silver whispered, and Ferrin was rather inclined to agree.

Louise took them to a sitting area in the back of the book-store, where she flopped into a comfortable armchair while Ferrin and Silver tried not to sit too close on the couch. "So. You've brought me children. *Before* asking me what you want."

"You already know it."

"Of course I do. Just look at them. But I want to know the details, Ferrin. Why on earth are you picking up children off the street in your spare time? Since when do you *have* spare time? And who is this?"

"Silver Crowe." Silver took her hand, and Louise looked from him to Ferrin, then narrowed her eyes in the all-too-familiar *what have we here* look.

Ferrin frowned at her. *Don't start.*

Louise primly crossed her legs. *Don't tell me what to do.*

Ferrin sighed. "I know this is an imposition, Louise, but you're the only one I trust to be fair. Other than Mother and Father, I suppose. But I know you were looking for help with the bookstore, and these two have a brother who might be in need of work."

"And in need of a place to stay?" Louise propped her chin on her hand. "Why? What happened to them?"

Silver cleared his throat. "I don't know how their parents died, but it was... it was bad. Philip is old enough to remember it, I think. Armand—the boy needing work—always goes pale at the sight of blood. Never said why, and I didn't want to ask."

"And now he might be in a difficult situation," Ferrin said. He explained the bare bones of it, leaving out the matter of the crown and the fact that Ferrin had walked into a den of thieves while Louise went quiet in her chair, staring at him.

"They could send him to sea for that, you know. Stealing in the palace." Her voice was soft, and Ferrin knew she was thinking of Wes. Wes, who was too clever by half but not in the way Ferrin and Louise were, in the way that helped them both navigate the lower city without falling into traps laid by charismatic "friends." Wes was starting to slip, spending too much time out at night and coming back with dirt on his trousers and a wild look in his eyes and their parents had finally decided enough was enough. He went off to sea when he was only thirteen and came back a few years later with a uniform, a medal, and a cool, detached manner that nearly brought Louise to tears. He'd left for the sea again three weeks later.

"He could end up in prison, as well," Silver said. "He has no one to pay his way out."

"Is he still being held right now?" Louise lowered her voice, leaning in.

"Ah. Yes. They should be done with him soon. Done questioning," Ferrin added when both Silver and Louise looked at him with alarm. "I can put in a request to have his holding fee waived."

Louise stood. "That won't be necessary."

"What?" Silver looked from Ferrin to his sister, brows raised. "I'm sorry, I don't understand."

Louise pushed her hair over her shoulder, and her voice rang with dominance. "When someone is held by the crown, their employer can request a release on their behalf. Since this boy—"

"Armand," Silver said in a dazed voice.

"—Armand, is currently working part-time in my shop as of...half a minute ago, I am perfectly within my rights to have him released into my custody."

"That's kind of fucked up, though," Silver said, "that your

employer can just...I don't know, make you come back because they need you to work."

"It's a system I have every intention to exploit at the moment, thank you," Louise said. "Watch the little ones while I'm gone. There's tea upstairs."

She disappeared up the steps that led to her upstairs apartment, and Ferrin and Silver sat on the couch in silence, staring at her empty chair.

"No wonder you're a guard captain," Silver said. "What are your parents' jobs? Emperor?"

Ferrin huffed out a soft laugh. "Carpenter and a street-cleaner, actually."

Silver sighed, sinking into the couch, and Ferrin patted his hand. He'd forgotten how single-minded Louise could get at times. Between her, the theft of the crown, the guild, and Ferrin's own deplorable behavior, he supposed Silver was exhausted.

Louise strode back down the steps in a lovely crimson gown, which Ferrin recognized as the one she always wore when she wanted to intimidate the life out of someone. Silver stared at her, and Violette, who had come round to show Silver her new book, gasped.

"You *are* a witch."

"A good one, I hope," Louise said and crouched down to look Violette in the eyes. "I'm going to fetch your brother, and we're all going to have a nice long talk, but while you wait for him, why don't you and Philip stay here? I have two bedrooms to spare, and since I'm a witch, you'll be quite safe."

Violette stared down at her feet for a moment, then nodded. "That makes sense."

"Thought so. Back soon, loves!" Louise waved her fingers at the lot of them as she made for the door, leaving Ferrin and Silver alone with the children.

Philip and Violette seemed utterly unbothered by staying in a supposed witch's house. "We've lived everywhere," Philip said as Ferrin unlocked Louise's apartment door and let them in. "One time, we even stayed in this old abandoned house owned by some rich noble who ran away, and we put on all his clothes and pretended to have a dinner party."

"And the food was imaginary, and Armie and Philip had a sword fight on the table and *broke* it."

"You don't say." Ferrin helped Silver wrangle the children into the spare room, forgetting entirely that children usually needed baths before bed, and left them thumbing through a picture book together while Cuddles walked back and forth over their legs, unsure where to sleep.

"I'm making you tea," Silver said as Ferrin collapsed on Louise's drawing room couch. "Actually, I'm making myself tea, but you're invited."

"Gallant of you," Ferrin murmured, rubbing his temples. Silver hesitated, and Ferrin thought of him pinned to the wall, obediently looking down, so eager to submit. He thought of the way Silver always walked at his heels, how he waited before Ferrin and Louise sat to take a seat on the couch himself. He wondered what Silver would look like at his feet, asking permission to join him on the couch, to touch him, to speak. All it would take would be a hand on his neck to make him eager for it, just a touch, a gesture of command.

"Do you." Silver swallowed audibly. "Would you *like* tea?"

"Good boy for asking," Ferrin said without thinking, and Silver flushed pink to his ears. "Ah. I shouldn't have."

"I don't mind." Silver blinked slowly, like a cat. "Is there...anything else you want, or..."

Ferrin regarded Silver. It had been a long day. That morning, he'd thought of Silver as yet another face in a sea of them, a competent tailor but not a member of the circle Ferrin usually had to navigate. Then he was a thief and a man who spoke passionately about the poor who slipped through the cracks in Staria, then a breathless, earnest submissive squirming in Ferrin's grip.

"I'm not in the habit of wanting things," Ferrin said, which was a lie. He just couldn't bring himself to *have* anything, not when the palace was his life. Not when he came home to an empty house and put his uniform in the same place it always was, everything in order, everything efficient, with no room for anything else.

"But if you were." Silver swayed as though he wanted to go to his knees. "What would you want?"

"Right now?" Ferrin sighed. He couldn't do this. He had a job to do, and he'd already put too much at risk. "Tea would be enough."

He looked away before Silver's face could fall and pinched his brow as Silver ran off to make tea. Now he was being a monster again. Forbidding and strict, just as he'd been with Wes the night his little brother tried to run away from home. He'd come to Ferrin with a suitcase and money he probably got from his so-called friends, desperate to escape the navy and sure that his older brother would do the right thing and help him skip town.

So Ferrin did the right thing and woke their parents.

He'd been doing the right thing, the *respectable* thing, his entire life, and now it left him here, with a stolen crown, a den of thieves down the street, orphaned kids living off his sister's charity, and a pretty submissive who deserved better than a man who would turn him down for a cup of tea.

Silver came back with two cups and a sheepish expression, and before he could open his mouth to apologize, Ferrin said, "don't. You did nothing wrong."

"You know who you're saying that to, yeah?" Silver sat down

next to him, and Ferrin took his cup. It was too sweet, but he wasn't about to admit it, so he drank it fast and settled on the couch in awkward silence.

He tried to think of what to say. He wasn't the best at giving romantic advice—it wasn't exactly in his job description—and he felt that anything he did say would come out wrong.

"Look," he said after a while. "Maybe, in the words of my brother, I'm a bit of an ass."

Silence. He turned and found Silver asleep in the corner of the couch, legs tucked up to his chest, one arm slung over his head. It was ridiculous and oddly endearing, and Ferrin got up to unfold one of the quilts from his sister's linen closet. He draped it over Silver, who instinctively hugged it close, and left to clean their cups.

Chapter Four

One benefit to keeping a regular routine was that even when he was sleeping on his sister's couch, Ferrin woke before dawn.

Someone had redistributed the quilts in the night, draping one over Ferrin's shoulders and adding a second to Silver's. Silver was curled up in a ball, his hair a mess and his mouth slightly open, and Ferrin stared at him for a moment before adding his own quilt to the pile.

It was odd, walking through his sister's house in the early morning. He rarely stayed the night—rarely visited, if he was being honest with himself—and while they'd been close as children, it was because their parents had hammered it home as their responsibility.

"Your siblings come first," their father had said when Louise had thrown Ferrin under the metaphorical cart for breaking their mother's music box. "Even before us. Before your country. Before anything."

But then they'd grown up, hadn't they, and priorities shifted. Louise was doing well enough on her own, and Wes—well, Wes was all right. It had turned out for the best in the end. Or that's what they'd told each other.

Ferrin opened the door to Louise's kitchen, and Armand turned to stare at him, halfway through shoving a lump of pumpkin bread down his shirt.

"C—captain."

"Not on duty yet," Ferrin said. "Put that down; it ain't healthy for breakfast, not the way Louise makes it."

"I wasn't taking it," Armand said. He set the bread back down, looked at the door, and sat at the kitchen table with his shoulders hunched like a crow.

"All right. I'm making eggs. How do you like them?"

Armand stared at him, and Ferrin gestured to the icebox. "Uh. On toast?"

Ferrin nodded and took out the eggs. He'd have to give Louise a stipend for taking care of the kids. Except she'd probably hand it right back. "So you met my sister last night. How'd that go?"

Armand looked down at his hands. "Made me take a bath."

"Yeah, she would." Ferrin eyed him as he took out the proper brown bread, slightly sweet and studded with nuts. Armand did look cleaner, and his hair had the disheveled look of someone who slept on it wet. "She talk to you at all?"

"Yeah. Said I'm working for her, so the crown's gotta let me out of jail." Armand frowned. "But people do stuff like this, you know. They do it all the time."

"Stuff like what?"

Armand gave him a hard look. "Rich folks say things like, come inside, you'll be our kids now. And you eat nice, maybe, and they give you good clothes, but then you find out what they really want. I ain't letting Phillip and Violette get caught up in that."

Ferrin cracked the egg, keeping his voice level. "But you

did? Got caught up in it?" Armand said nothing, which was enough. "You think my sister's like that?"

"They're always nice at first."

Ferrin paused. He knew Armand might not believe him, even so, and he probably had no reason to. The city guard should have been there to help Armand and his siblings, but they would have pushed Armand aside if he'd gone to them. Ferrin knew that much. Just cleaning out corruption in the palace guard had taken him the better part of a decade.

"I was about your age when I joined the guard. How old are you? Fifteen? Sixteen?"

"I guess."

Ferrin checked the toast, which was browning slightly. "I started as a trainee in the city guard. All palace guards used to start there before I became captain. They had a tradition, see. Called it *earning your way*. You had to do whatever the senior officers told you. Sometimes it was shining shoes or running errands. Sometimes it wasn't. People took advantage, turned it into a sick game. They'd see how far they could push you before you broke."

"Yeah, but they wouldn't do it to you; you're different." Armand waited and said, "but you're different."

"I was sixteen, and I wanted to be a guard in the palace. I doubt I was the first to be beaten in a hazing. I thought I could handle it. Louise saw the bruises one night. She got the officer's name out of me. Then she left the house. The next day, he..." Ferrin shrugged. "He didn't show up for muster."

Armand's eyes widened. "She *killed* him?"

"No. But he didn't go back to the guard, either. That's the kind of woman my sister is. She rescues snakes and shouts down nobles who ride their carriages too fast in the street. She made a splint for a mouse once. She went to the king to get *you* out, and she didn't even know what you looked like. I'm not asking you to believe me because maybe you don't have a reason to right now, but I'm asking you to give her a chance. Stick with her, and she'll fight for you."

"Like a chicken," Armand said. Ferrin raised a brow at him. "Sometimes, if you put a snake in with a mama chicken, it'll rip the thing to pieces. I heard about it from a friend."

"Yeah. Like that." Ferrin slipped the toad in the hole onto a plate and handed it to Armand, who immediately reached for the salt. "So give her a few days. She'll keep you safe."

"Maybe we'll stick around. If she's paying," Armand added. "And food is free. But why'd you become a guard if they were shit, though?"

Ferrin shrugged. "I thought maybe they shouldn't be. Did they beat you in the cells? Torture you? Threaten you?"

"No, they gave me something to drink and asked me a lot of questions I didn't understand. Like who asked me to steal from the palace. Which I didn't, and no one asked me."

Ferrin considered letting him sit in the enormity of that lie, but judging by the look on Armand's face, the boy clearly knew Ferrin hadn't bought it. "Really."

"And even if the palace guards are fine, the city guards'll ship you off to the quarries as soon as look at you. Or they used to. They're not allowed to take as many anymore, so now they just kick us around a little."

Ferrin didn't like the sound of that. "City guard isn't under me, unfortunately."

"Sucks for us, huh."

Ferrin had a feeling he wasn't going to get anything out of Armand yet. Making him eggs on toast and talking about corruption in the city guard wasn't enough to endear him to a street thief. He had to give him time, which Ferrin had in precious supply. So he'd have to leave him with Louise for a day or two, let him relax, no longer on edge from his stay in the palace cells.

"Is that Ferrin at the stove?" Louise appeared at the doorway, already dressed, her eyes shining. "Don't go; I want to remember this for posterity. I didn't think you knew how to cook."

"I've been living alone for decades, Lou."

"That means nothing. Armand, have some pumpkin bread. It's like dessert for breakfast."

Despite her teasing, Louise did take over at the stove as soon as the other children were up, clearly unused to having anyone else in her kitchen. Ferrin took two plates out to the drawing room, where Silver was slowly blinking himself awake, and laid them down on the tea table.

"I have to go to work soon," he said as Silver extricated himself from the quilts. "There were still others near the...thing that was stolen. I'll need to make inquiries."

"Fontaine and Rousseau," Silver said. "And the maid."

Ferrin was mildly impressed that Silver remembered. "Yes. They could have seen something or been a part of it."

"I have a fitting with Lord Rousseau this afternoon," Silver said, looking anywhere but at Ferrin. "I could...you know. Talk to him. I'm good at reading people."

"Just be discreet," Ferrin said. "But thank you. Your cooperation—it isn't necessary, but I'm grateful for it."

Silver looked down. "I know I'm complicating things."

"No, it isn't that. I mean, you went out of your way and put yourself at risk—I mean to say thank you, Silver. I'm thanking you."

Silver smiled a little. "You're welcome. And thanks for giving Armand a chance. For convincing him to stay here."

Ferrin went quiet, and Silver blushed to his ears. "You heard that? I thought you were asleep."

"Your voices echoed," Silver said and shoved a piece of toast in his mouth as though to silence himself.

Ferrin wondered if he should say something. Most of the guard from Ferrin's generation didn't talk about hazing. Most treated it as either an unfortunate rough patch or "a bit of fun," and Ferrin still had to crack down now and then when someone inevitably tried to reinvent it. He'd been mortified when Louise found out, but she didn't let that stand.

"People need to treat you with dignity," she'd told him, brimming with righteous outrage. "That's what anyone deserves."

If *she'd* become a guard, she would have cleaned the palace up in a week.

"I wonder if they're still like that." Silver glanced at Ferrin sidelong. "The city guards."

"I don't doubt it. Their current captain was one of my seniors." Ferrin scowled at his plate. Marcel Clemens was a pompous, slithery little bully who made himself out to be a paragon of virtue. No inspector would catch him subtly egging on his subordinates or ignoring Ferrin's reports of palace staff being harassed by the city guard—which was as much as Ferrin was able to do in his position. He had a perfect manner and the polished speech of a son of well-to-do merchants, and when Ferrin was a rookie, he used to purposely make a mess when he knew Ferrin was scheduled to clean. He still treated Ferrin like he was a dirty, lower-class street kid, though he kept his snide remarks and meaningful looks far from the crown's notice.

"No wonder they're all jerks," Silver said. "You should send your sister after them."

Ferrin laughed. "You're right. Maybe I should. But we both have work to do. If you don't mind, I can escort you to the palace."

Silver blushed again, and Ferrin wondered if he'd overstepped. He remembered Silver's dejected look last night and supposed it still stung. But Silver just nodded and went back to his breakfast.

Louise was drilling Armand in the function of a bookshop by the time they were done. She gave Ferrin a look—*we're not done talking about this*—but was too busy showing Phillip how to do the washing-up to reject Ferrin when he slipped a handful of coins in her pocket.

The sun was just rising as they made their way to the palace. Duciel was a different city in the early morning, but Ferrin was far more interested in Silver, who went from a contemplative silence to keen awareness in a matter of moments. It was as though he, too, came alive with the sun, and Ferrin let his usual pace falter as Silver pointed out shops he liked and the way people were easier to recognize in the morning.

"People can suppress themselves, sometimes," Silver said. "Like wearing a cloak over a gown. You can see the general shape of them, but they're easier to read when they're off guard."

"The way you talk, it sounds like magic."

"It is, sort of. I can't really explain it right, but I've always had it. It's like people have a unique... mark."

"Does it ever tell you if they're trustworthy?"

Silver frowned slightly. "Not really. If you say things like, I don't know, forest ponds or the general impression of a rainstorm is trustworthy, you're putting a lot of weight on an abstract concept."

Ferrin, who rarely dealt with abstract concepts on the whole, just nodded.

"Shouldn't we stop by your place for clothes?"

Ferrin shrugged. "I keep spares in the barracks. I'm practically living there, right now."

"And that's...healthy?"

Ferrin didn't have the foggiest idea why Silver was giving him such a concerned look. "The building is up to code."

Silver's shoulders sagged. "Right. Okay."

They parted ways at the gates, where, thankfully, Ferrin's newest recruits knew enough to check *everyone* before letting them in. They were sheepish about it when they asked Ferrin for his title, sure, but it was necessary, particularly with thieves traipsing about with stolen crowns in their pockets.

He threw himself into his morning duties, going over the roster while he showered and changed, and sifted through a number of alarming notes on his desk. The most urgent came from Sabre de Valois, Prince Adrien's left hand and the inheritor of Isiodore de Mortain's army of spies—no doubt the theft rankled. He wanted Ferrin present when they questioned the maid, Hana, who'd been spotted near the throne room around the time of the theft.

She's from the lower city, Sabre had written. *She could use a familiar face.*

As though people in the lower city were automatically inclined to trust one another. Ferrin wondered if Sabre knew about the bakery thieves. That was the trouble with people like Sabre or Isiodore—they never revealed their full hands, even when it would be damn well convenient to do so. Ferrin tossed the note in the fire, waited until it burned properly, and went upstairs to speak to a maid about a crown.

* * *

Sabre de Valois met Ferrin in one of the small drawing rooms set aside for servants in the palace. There were dozens of them, a whole network of rooms and hallways the nobility never saw, but Sabre seemed quite at home there, sitting in a worn but serviceable chair with his reddish hair tied back and his expensive jacket abandoned by the door.

He was another symbol of Adrien's new reign, a noble who hated it, discarding the trappings of his own power as soon as he had the chance. Ferrin always felt vaguely uncomfortable around him since it had been Ferrin who arrested Sabre's family some years ago when the de Valois women decided to turn on the crown. It was an unpleasant business, and seeing Sabre at his lowest—shaking on the gallows, begging to hold his sister's hand—would always color Ferrin's image of him now. He would be the second most powerful man in Staria soon enough, and Ferrin knew full well that the crown was lucky he wasn't inclined to revenge.

"Captain." Sabre smiled and gestured to a tray of tea and biscuits. "Sit, please. This is an informal conversation."

Ah. Then he likely had no need for a guard unless an arrest was to be made. Ferrin sat on the opposite couch, and Sabre leaned in to pour the tea.

"What do you know about the maid so far?" Ferrin asked.

Sabre shrugged a shoulder. "Hana Lowering. She doesn't know anything was stolen yet—just that there was a situation we're still working out regarding her being turned away at the throne room. She's a professional—her family worked for the de Sartre's, and she spent a few summers in d'Hiver—they're cousins, of a sort," he added. "Then she went back to the palace to look after my suites. I thoroughly vetted her when she joined the staff, of course. Two sisters in the navy and, according to my agents, a sweetheart out of Staria. They write letters."

Ferrin nodded as though a maid with a beau had anything to do with a stolen crown. "No ties to any unsavory characters, then."

"Not unless you count the nobility." Sabre smiled into his

teacup. "Her first employer became a pirate, her second is rumored to be possessed, and her current employer is a whore."

"I wouldn't call you that."

"Who do you think commoners are more comfortable with, Captain?" Sabre's expression, which had been affable until now, hardened. "A noble who can upend their lives at a word, or a man who lives in a pleasure house?"

Ferrin would have said both were dangerous—a courtesan was not precisely someone to underestimate—but held his tongue. "They're not comfortable with guard captains."

"No, but I have a plan. Just sit there and look stern, and when you leave, I'll feed her biscuits and ask about her family. When we're done, I'll send you my notes the usual way."

Ferrin raised a brow. Isiodore, King Emile's spymaster, would not have taken such a roundabout manner, but then they *were* very different people. Sabre was playing to his strengths, using his submission—and his own mistreatment at the hands of the crown—to his advantage. "All right, then."

Sabre smiled again, all hardness gone from his eyes, and got up to fetch the maid. Which Isiodore also would not have done —the maid would already be there, probably kneeling on the rug and begging for clemency. Isiodore tended to have that effect on people.

Hana Lowering was a wide-set woman with eyes that looked just a little too large for her face and a mass of gold hair braided in a crown. She bowed to Ferrin, which was unnecessary, and smiled at Sabre when he led her to the best chair and handed her a cup of tea.

"Terrible business the other day, wasn't it?" Sabre asked. "How are you holding up? More sugar?"

"Oh! Thank you. I'm doing just fine, my lord. I'm surprised you're all taking it so seriously. How is his highness?"

My lord, Ferrin noticed, not *your grace*. Sabre added a cube of sugar to her tea. "He is unflappable as always. Someone found a puppy in the stables, and he insisted on being there when it was named."

"No, really?"

Ferrin leaned back, watching as Sabre effectively closed Ferrin out of the conversation. It had to be something he learned from his time living in the House of Onyx—he flirted with Hana like a trained courtesan, and she eased closer and closer to him, her careful cadence dropping as she sank into a comfortable chatter.

"Oh, damn, I forgot, have you met Captain Ferrin? He's investigating that business from the throne room, with that man?"

"Oh, yes, hello. You really should tell his highness to do something about him," Hana said, ignoring Ferrin completely. "I don't mind it so much, but the younger maids hate it when he's here."

Sabre gave Ferrin a confused look. "When Captain...Ferrin...is here?"

Hana laughed. "Not *him*, bless you. No, we're quite safe with Captain Ferrin. He has no interest in romance; everyone knows that." Ferrin was about to protest—really, this was taking it a step too far—when Hana leaned in toward Sabre and said, with all the confidence of a dear friend, "Besides. You asked about that man from yesterday? The one who turned me away from the throne room? Even though Lord Rousseau and Lady Fontaine were already inside, bold as you please. The man I mentioned was Captain Marcel, and let me tell you, he can say as many sweet things as he likes, but if he touches my bum again, he'll leave the palace with a missing hand."

Ferrin kept his expression straight only through a sheer force of will as Hana helpfully explained that she'd been heading to the throne room to cut through to a servant's corridor when Captain Marcel intervened, firmly turning her around with a smack on her rear for good measure.

"Which was unnecessary—even that sweetheart—" Hana stopped. "A noble, in the hallway, with a green cloak, he told him to leave off."

"Can you describe the noble at all?" Sabre asked while Ferrin imagined seven new ways to strangle Marcel for laying a hand on a member of the palace staff. "You recognized Fontaine and Rousseau, but not him?"

"Well, I saw them *before* I had to deal with the captain. The man in the cloak...he was... Tall? Dark haired? Pretty, I guess? I was so flustered, my lord."

That was that. Ferrin was going to slap the bastard with so many formal complaints he would *choke* on them because Ferrin would personally *stuff* the complaints down his *throat*—

"An olive green or darker?"

"I can't rightly say, my lord."

And when he was done, Ferrin was going to drag the bastard back to the palace and shove him into the compost pile behind the stables, see how *he* handled a little *light cleaning*—

"Captain?"

Ferrin snapped to attention. "Ah. Yes."

"That was the bell for the end of the hour, Captain," Sabre said, eyeing the door. Ferrin stood.

"Yes, of course. Ms. Lowering, I can issue an anonymous complaint on your behalf, and if this happens again..."

"Oh, yes, I know. You're the good sort, Captain; we all know that."

Ferrin tried not to feel as though he were fleeing the room. The palace was *his* domain—what right did Marcel have to give orders to the staff, let alone mistreat them? And why hadn't his presence been reported yesterday? What was he saying to Ferrin's own guards?

Well, he'd put a stop to *that*. Ferrin called an emergency muster, hammered it into his guards' heads that *no one* was above his orders but the king himself, and left the barracks feeling like he was caught in the middle of a storm, his dominance only barely held in check.

He didn't register that his body, operating mindlessly, had brought him to Silver's quarters until he was almost there. He stopped, staring at the plaque on the door, and was about to turn around and take his lunch in the barracks as usual when the door swung open.

Silver stood there, wide-eyed and fresh-faced, with a measuring tape over one shoulder and a colorful mess at his back. Ferrin tried to speak, but he couldn't put his thoughts to words. Was the palace safe to the staff? Had Ferrin done enough? Was it pointless? Was he doomed to fail every single aspect of his duty until Adrien was left without a crown and the servants without an advocate? And did the palace *really* think he had no interest in romance?

"Do you...want to come in?" Silver asked after a while.

"Yes," Ferrin said, finally. "I very much would."

* * *

Ferrin looked like he wanted to smack someone. Silver wished, with all the longing in his soul, that it was him.

That was silly, though. He'd given plenty of hints, hadn't he, that he wouldn't be averse to kneeling and letting Ferrin do whatever he wanted to him? Also, yeah, wow, they had other things they needed to focus on, but the look on Ferrin's face screamed *frustrated dominant,* and Silver's inner frustrated submissive perked up like a cat spotting a mouse—or maybe it was the mouse. Who had time for complicated analogies right now?

Silver stepped back when he realized he was staring at Ferrin like a complete fool and smiled brightly. That probably didn't make him look less wild, but oh well. "What happened?"

Ferrin sighed. "Other people's incompetence, mostly."

Silver wondered if anyone ever saw Ferrin like this; he was usually so calm and collected, and it was kind of nice to know the unflappable guard captain got annoyed on occasion. And it was really nice to be allowed to see it, like some kind of gift.

Or maybe you just annoy him, a little voice murmured, and Silver pushed it down. Now wasn't the time for his usual self-doubts. "Need to talk about it?"

Ferrin blinked, then smiled. "No, it's—a captain making a nuisance of himself. Not one of mine. Someone who shouldn't have his job and who abuses his authority."

"Ah." Silver snorted. "Captain Marcel?"

Ferrin's smile turned into a grin, and it was so attractive Silver wanted to lay on the floor and stare at the ceiling for two or three hours and *die.* "How'd you know?"

"He comes in here and orders stuff," Silver said, shrugging. "It's always expensive for the sake of being expensive and usually tacky. And he doesn't listen to my suggestions, just snaps out orders like he's a noble and then never stands still for his measurements. He sent a coat back once because the sleeve was a centimeter short, and like, sure, buddy, you have to let me measure, that's what *happens* if you 'eyeball' it and your eyeballs suck, I guess."

Ferrin laughed. "Did you tell him that?"

"Nah, he has that. *I'll hide a brooch in your boot and turn you in* kinda look, you know? I thought it, though. Loudly. But I'll tell you something about his aura—he thinks he's a gold-and-silk guy but really? Tin and scrap leather. If that."

"Ah," Ferrin said, clearly biting back another laugh. "But I thought you said an aura wasn't an indication of morality?"

"It's not, but in his case, plenty of other things *are*. Like screaming at me about a cuff and demanding I fix it for free, immediately, even though I was in the middle of a fitting with someone else."

"He's a pompous ass, and I'm not surprised to hear he acts that way with everyone." Ferrin made a face. "I'd think he was a suspect, but he'd never do his own dirty work."

"Probably not," Silver agreed. He bounced on his heels and went over to an overstuffed chair in the corner, which was, of course, covered in bolts of cloth, an extra measuring tape, and a pincushion. He moved everything and indicated the chair. "Have a seat. Um. If you want."

To his surprise, Ferrin sat, leaning forward with his elbows on his knees. "For as chaotic as this space is, it's surprisingly calm."

"Fabrics are nice, that's why." Silver turned, grabbed a scrap of soft velvet, and held it out to Ferrin. "Pet that; it's like a cat, but it won't jump off your lap when there's a loud noise."

Ferrin stared at him, and Silver's ears went hot, but then he took the fabric and dragged his fingers over it. Silver's mouth went dry, but he pasted on a pleasant smile and said, "See? Nice, huh?"

"Yes," Ferrin said, his smile gone, dark eyes intent on Silver's face while he continued to stroke the small fabric square. "Very."

Silver's own smile faded as they stared at each other, the tension kicking up a notch. Silver wanted to kneel there and let Ferrin pet *him*—and in fact, he was half a second away from saying something absurd like *my hair is also nice, want to pet that? My dick, too. It's soft. Velvety.*

"Do you, um. Want some tea?" A less-fun suggestion but slightly less unhinged-sounding.

Ferrin shook his head. "No. Would you mind—I'm sorry. I shouldn't ask."

Silver suddenly couldn't breathe. "It's—go ahead, ask. You can, it's fine." *Please let this question be about your dick, or your hand and my ass—*

"Would you please kneel?" Ferrin asked after a moment, and every single nerve in Silver's body went up like those fire-crackers he and his best friend Rowan used to shoot off at home in Diabolos.

Whatever expression was on his face made Ferrin glance away. "I'm sorry. I shouldn't have asked you to do that—"

Silver's knees hit the floor before he finished and took back the order. "Yeah, of course." The second he did it, knelt for Ferrin, the wild, restless feeling in his head seemed to ease, and while he was still ridiculously turned on, he could breathe easier and felt decidedly less jittery. "That's—I kinda needed to kneel, actually."

"You shouldn't neglect these things," Ferrin said sternly, then smiled a little wryly. "Which, I know, is very *do as I say, not as I do* of me."

I will literally do whatever you say; try me. "Yeah." Silver realized his hands were behind his back, and when Ferrin saw that, his eyes flashed. "It helps when I have, um, fittings and stuff. Sometimes."

Ferrin was still absently touching that little velvet square, which Silver might, possibly, sleep with for the rest of his life. "Not with men like Captain Marcel, I'm assuming."

Silver chuckled, and it was only a little strained. "Yeah, no. Not for him. He's a dom but not the kind I'd ever kneel for."

"Good." Ferrin's eyes narrowed thoughtfully. "Shoulders back. There." He sighed, and it really did seem like some of his tension abated. "I, ah. Protocol relaxes me."

Silver had to swallow before he could speak. "I bet. With your, um. Job."

"I wasn't talking about my job." Ferrin reached out, and Silver's heart started beating faster as Ferrins' fingers tipped his chin up. "Thank you for this. I've felt entirely out of control too many times today."

"Dominants hate that, so I hear," Silver joked weakly as Ferrin drew his hand back.

"This one certainly does." Ferrin kept looking at him, and his approval was like a warm bath on a cold morning, or a delicious hot cup of chocolate, or a thousand other things that made heat spread pleasantly through Silver's veins.

"Been awhile for you, too, huh?" Silver was trying to get up the nerve to offer more of it, that he would be happy to follow any and all protocols Ferrin wanted to give him—and they didn't have to even involve his dick or his hand on Silver's backside. He wasn't one for pain, but he did like being spanked. Something about the loss of control, and the shame of it, made him settle like nothing else.

"It has," Ferrin said. He drew in a breath, and Silver leaned forward a bit on instinct before quickly reverting back to proper form. That got a soft sound from Ferrin, taking away whatever he was going to say, and Silver knew it was now or never.

"Me, too. If you wanted me to, I could—submit to you." He could barely get the words out, but he did, and he didn't lower his gaze, either.

Something hungry flashed in Ferrin's dark gaze. "You are."

Silver closed his eyes and only just managed to bite back a moan. "More. I could do...more. Of that. Submitting, I mean. If you wanted."

"Look at me," Ferrin said, and his voice was so full of dominance that Silver couldn't have done anything else.

He opened his eyes, and Ferrin was staring at him like a

starving man at a banquet. "Yes, sir?" Silver was too turned on, too *desperate*, to be embarrassed at the title. Ferrin *was* a captain.

"I do want," Ferrin said, and all of Silver's remaining brain power fizzled into a quiet hum.

"Then tell me what to do," Silver said after he found enough breath to speak.

Ferrin drew in another breath...and then there was an enthusiastic pounding on the door, which was not at all the enthusiastic pounding Silver wanted at the moment.

Damn and blast. He'd forgotten his fitting with Count Rousseau, who was here on *time*, and couldn't he have been waylaid for...ever, maybe? A rogue bear let loose in the palace? Which wasn't nice; just because Rousseau *looked* kind of shady and like he was up to something didn't mean he *was*. He was an all-right client if a little bombastic and far too fond of shades that did nothing for his particular coloring.

Silver wasn't under, but he was in headspace enough that when the knock came again, he glanced at Ferrin for permission to break protocol.

Ferrin gave a terse nod—at least he looked as annoyed by the interruption as Silver was—and Silver got to his feet with a little hop, hurrying over to the door to open it.

"There you are, lad, never say I'm early! I'm fashionably late as a rule," Rousseau announced, sweeping in. He was wearing too much lace and the fuchsia jacket he'd insisted Silver make for him, which would have looked nice on, say, Ferrin or Bazyli Drakos, but did nothing for the ginger-haired Rousseau. And the buttons were brass with emerald, and instead of his shirt being white, it was a pale yellow—he looked like one of the pirates back in Diabolos, the kind who wore dramatic and color-clashing clothing because they were pirates, and it was part of the aesthetic.

"You're fine, m'lord," Silver said with a hasty bob of his head, moving aside as the tornado that was Count Rousseau swept through the room. He tossed his hat at a table—the hat was a little too large for his head, and maybe the hatter had a stronger personality and ability to tell nobles *no* than Silver did because it was a normal shade of blue—and missed, and of course, didn't bother to go pick it up.

Nobles. This one was less irritating than some, even given his outlandish fashion sense and apparent color-blindness, but he still thought it was someone else's job to pick up after him. Which it was, but that person was not here, and Silver's job was to make clothes, not play valet and make up for Rousseau's poor aim.

"Oh, ho! Captain Ferrin! Here to get something tailored, are you?"

He was going to get the tailor until you showed up.

Ferrin had risen to his feet and gave a respectful nod to Count Rousseau, all hints of his earlier dominance and interest carefully masked. "Count Rousseau. Yes. A coat for His Highness' coronation."

Rousseau gave a much-too-loud laugh and waved a hand. "You're lucky that Master Crowe can fit you in, no pun intended, of course—I tried to get a coronation suit, and this poor lad said he was just too busy!"

"I have a role to play in the ceremony," Ferrin said smoothly. "His Majesty insisted."

Rousseau chuckled. "He would, wouldn't he? For a man who cares little for his own wardrobe, he at least appreciates talent in that area when he sees it. Our Master Crowe here is all the rage with the fashionable elite."

Please don't let them think I dress you, or I won't be, anymore. Silver put on his best service-worker smile and said carefully, "Thank you, my lord."

"Think nothing of it! I would wear this *wonderful* suit you're making me to the coronation, but I'm wearing it to my party, and you know I couldn't possibly wear the same thing *twice* in front of so many of my peers."

Of course not. He'd spend enough money to send Armand's siblings to university in Gerakia on a coat he'd only wear once. Silver had to remind himself that this was his job and not think too hard about it—these nobles were his clients. It was only that sometimes, it felt like trading one type of theft for another.

Silver went to get Rousseau's suit jacket from the mannequin where it was hanging—mostly finished—with only a few alterations left. This one was equally as...eye-catching...only in a shade of bright, robin's egg blue that at least looked better with his coloring than his initial request for violet.

"Captain Ferrin, you know, I did send you an invitation to my ball, but it would seem you did not respond." Rousseau clicked his tongue. "Please tell me that was a dreadful oversight; you do look so dashing in your uniform."

Silver almost knocked over another form, then reminded himself that was true, and Ferrin should be admired for his hotness by everyone.

"I do not often attend parties," Ferrin said. "Unless I am accompanying His Majesty."

"Oh, bah, the king never does attend anyone's parties... except that birthday party for the actress, did you hear about that?" Rousseau gossiped as Silver went to drape the coat on his shoulders, patiently waiting for him to stop twisting about as he stood before the mirrors. Rousseau had ginger hair that was thinning on top and a mustache that really should have chosen to go elsewhere on his head, and he was a bit fuller through the middle than the last time he'd shown up for a fitting.

"Everyone will be there," Rousseau continued as Silver discreetly made a note to let out a few seams on the side. "Viscountess Fontaine and I are doing this together, you know, and she knows *everyone*, so it shall be quite lively! You really should make an appearance, you're not a noble, but you do the fine job of guarding us, so the added safety with so many wealthy, influential people there certainly won't go amiss."

Of course, that's why he wanted Ferrin there—or maybe not, maybe it was just the added prestige of the king's guard captain, who knew? It could be both. Rousseau was as pompous as a pampered dog that lived in a lady's handbag, but he was harmless enough. Unlike the odious Captain Marcel, he tended toward more casual offensiveness than outright rudeness. Like tossing the hat on the ground and not noticing. Marcel probably would have demanded Silver pay for it to be cleaned for touching the floor.

Ferrin was giving Rousseau a speculative look, which Rousseau was too busy admiring himself in the mirror to notice. "Viscountess Fontaine?"

"Yes, yes, you know she has that whole *fondness* for oddities, yes? She's recently had the most wonderful idea for something to auction!" Rousseau beamed. "Those are terribly fun, all the excitement of bidding and, of course, winning." He chuckled.

"Oddities," Ferrin repeated slowly. "What sort of oddities?"

"Oh, well, I can't very well *tell* you, can I? What fun is that? No, no, you simply *must* come. I think you'll enjoy seeing what we have on offer—very exclusive, you know. The invitation was for you and a plus one, but you don't have a submissive, do you?"

"No," Ferrin said. "I don't."

He was about to, and then you knocked on the door. Silver took a pin out of the coat and shifted it a bit to get the measurement right.

"What a shame, a handsome man like you," Rousseau purred. "You should absolutely make a point to attend, then. We might find one for you, or if you like, you can be my escort—oh, dear, Master Crowe! Do watch where you're sticking that pin!"

"Sorry," Silver said sweetly.

Ferrin coughed into his fist. "Thank you for the invitation. I might attend after all—you said I could bring someone?"

Rousseau looked momentarily dejected, which, fair, Silver knew how that felt. But he brightened immediately and nodded. "Certainly. Send the invitation back, so we know to expect you, and...do bring money with you; you do get paid, don't you?"

"I—yes," Ferrin said, and this time, it was Silver who had to duck his head and hide a laugh.

"The items on auction range in price, but they're all expensive, and some are *very* rare," Rousseau continued as Silver made the last of his modifications. He finished up making a few notes while Rousseau continued to talk Ferrin's ear off, and as Rousseau swept toward the door, Silver went to get his hat off the floor because it was a nice hat and deserved better. And it made Rousseau's hair look better, covering it up like that.

Before he could, Ferrin stepped by him and neatly reached down to pick the hat up and offer it to Count Rousseau. "You seem to have missed the hat rack. It's over there. For next time."

Well, if Silver didn't want to blow him *before*.... He was pretty sure there were actual stars in his eyes as Rousseau beamed and put the hat on, likely forgetting that the hat rack existed before the door closed behind him,

There was a moment of silence, and then Ferrin asked, "Want to go to a party with me?"

"No," Silver said, then hurriedly, "I mean, yeah, but...not that guy's?"

"Yes. Earlier, de Valois was questioning a maid, and she said she saw two figures near the crown. Want to guess who it was?"

Silver stared at him. "I'm guessing Rousseau and lady whats-her-name? Fountain?"

"Fontaine, yes," Ferrin said and smiled like a shark. "And you heard what he said about the priceless item on auction?"

"You think he's selling the *First Crown of Staria* at a party?" Silver scowled. "I mean, sure, that sounds like something he'd do, but...would he risk the king's displeasure or, like, jail?"

"Bold of you to assume he fears going to jail. And I don't know, but it's the first lead we have. So, will you accompany me?"

Silver would much rather get back to what they were about to do before...but it was clear Ferrin was distracted, and Silver understood why. It was a personal affront for the king's guard captain to have something as priceless as the crown go missing, and if it turned up at a fancy noble party...

"Sure," Silver said and smiled slightly. "I'll even dress myself up for the occasion. And you, if you want."

"I'll send word with the details," Ferrin said and gave him a short bow. "And I haven't forgotten what we discussed. It isn't contingent on your helping me, but I *would* like the help. You're an excellent judge of character."

It was a compliment, and Silver knew it—but right now, he'd rather be kneeling with Ferrin's cock in his mouth and his hand in Silver's hair, making him do it *just right*. But hey, he'd take what he could get.

Chapter Five

Ferrin hated parties.

Even when he was a boy and his parents would gather with their neighbors to turn the street into an exclusive buffet, Ferrin couldn't quite manage it. Wes and Louise would run about, laughing with friends and speaking animatedly with older neighbors, but Ferrin would turn into a polite, distant block of wood. His father used to laugh and call him "our little big man" since everyone thought Ferrin was just too eager to be an adult and couldn't quite get it right. The truth was, Ferrin just didn't know what to say or do, so he reverted to the only thing that worked; stiff, painful politeness.

He was already half petrified when Silver came to his door. Ferrin had changed into a new dress uniform, which a neighbor girl pressed for him for a few coppers, and his boots and buckles gleamed in desperate self-defense. When he came to the door, Silver took a moment to stare at him, taking it all in.

"We don't have to go," he said, and for a brief, wild moment, Ferrin wanted to kiss him just for that.

"No. Unofficial auctions are reason enough." He looked down at Silver, who was dressed in a fetching blue and gray suit that hugged his frame and almost complimented Ferrin's uniform. It was made out of...silk, maybe. He wasn't sure. He had never paid attention to fabrics before.

Now, he wondered if he ought to.

"What's that made of?" he asked nonsensically, and Silver looked down at his shirt.

"Cotton? It's just woven really fine, so you'd never know. But the strips around the sleeve are silk; feel the difference."

Ferrin took Silver's arm by the wrist, feeling the difference between the silk and fine cotton, the smooth needlework that made the wrist cuffs glimmer with images of silvery fish. He thought of Silver in his office, stitching carefully, all that erratic energy focused like the path of a sword.

"It's good work," Ferrin said softly and let go. Silver gasped in a little breath as though he'd been holding it. "We should go."

Silver made an incomprehensible sound in the back of his throat, and Ferrin smiled.

They stopped a public carriage trundling through the street because Ferrin knew enough about types like Lord Rousseau to suspect they'd spend all night tittering if he walked. "I should tell you, Silver, anyone who is up to something suspicious will want to keep me out of sight all evening. Watch the crowd, if you can. If people seem to be scurrying up ahead—trying to clean up, or closing doors, that kind of thing—let me know by— mm. We need a signal."

"I'll play with my cuff," Silver said and made a gesture with his hand. "Two fingers down means danger. One means follow. Three means run."

"Thieves' signals?" Ferrin raised an eyebrow, and Silver shrugged.

"I'm full of useful tricks," he said and immediately pressed his mouth together, blushing hotly. Ferrin leaned in, touching his arm as the carriage rolled to a halt.

"As much as I'm sure you are, I'd prefer we didn't test them here. Lord Rousseau's decor is famous in the court for being... alarming, and I'd rather not associate you with his stuffed ferret armoire."

"His what now?"

"You'll see."

"No, you can't leave me in the lurch with that, Captain," Silver said, slipping out of the carriage so he could hold out a hand for Ferrin. Ferrin, who had never been helped out of a carriage in his life, suppressed a smile and took it. "People don't just say stuffed ferret armoire and then go around like normal."

"I ain't saying it's normal," Ferrin murmured, speaking into Silver's ear. He straightened. Lord Rousseau's house was gaudy and ancient all at once. As one of the oldest noble families in Staria, he had the typical sunburst imagery carved into the pillars and doors, but as a Rousseau, he also had nymphs shoved over windows and satyrs fucking each other in marble. Silver stopped to stare at a fountain shaped like a woman having a little too much excitement on a giant fish, and Ferrin sighed.

"Somehow, I'm not surprised," Silver said.

Ferrin was back in his block of wood status as soon as they reached the door, where a woman in a patchwork gown and a rabbit mask wrote their names down on a little book.

"Oh, Captain Leonhart." Her lashes fluttered under the mask. "Fancy seeing you here! The court will speak of nothing else." Unless they found out about the crown being missing, of course. Ferrin nodded. "And... Silver. Just Silver? Is that a stage name? You know you can simply buy your own, Captain."

Ferrin's brows lowered, and Silver reached for his hand. "I'm one of a kind."

"I'm sure you are. Ask Lord Rousseau about the tiger, Captain; he needs someone dashing to shake a sword at it tonight."

"A... tiger..." Silver squinted at Ferrin, and Ferrin shrugged as they stepped inside.

"If it's real, it's a breach of the law."

"Please don't arrest a tiger," Silver whispered. If Ferrin weren't already mostly petrified, he would have laughed.

Lord Rousseau was, predictably, in the middle of the main drawing room, standing on a table. Ferrin noticed Silver's wince at the state of his clothes, which were...mismatched, to say the least, but he was holding up an enormous golden urn bursting with sunflowers.

"Taken from the god of desire's throne room itself," he was saying. "Take a petal, everyone; it's good luck. Go on."

"What?" Silver's voice was faint.

"I have no notion," Ferrin whispered back.

"I do, though." Silver was frowning slightly. "We talk about the god of desire in Diabolos a lot—he's kind of like an unofficial patron of pirates, I guess. And by talk, I mean we don't talk. You don't mention him, don't say his name, and definitely don't ask him for anything. This is like someone pouring a barrel of oil and striking a match."

"Then we should avoid the sunflowers," Ferrin said and steered Silver away toward the edge of the room. None of the nobles Ferrin cared for were there, of course, since they tended to be at least halfway sensible, but there was a quiet corner near a statue of a man with...oh, dear. That was a penis wrapped around his leg like a snake.

"Please note that I'm showing so much restraint right now," Silver said, mouth quivering.

"Noted."

"And the auction is in thirty minutes, people, don't forget! In the sunset room!" Lord Rousseau jumped down from the table, and there was a crack of a bottle being popped.

"We should find the sunset room, I think," Ferrin murmured.

Silver nodded, staring at the crowd, and gestured to a side door, where a number of servants were filing in and out. Ferrin nodded shortly and started in that direction, smiling painfully at the nobles who exclaimed or tried to call his name as he passed.

Then he heard it.

"Is that the little lion cub?" Ferrin stiffened for a moment, grabbed Silver's hand, and kept walking. "I say, Ferrin? Is that you, old boy?"

"No, it isn't," Ferrin breathed, but it was too late. A tall, sturdy-looking man with a swoop of blond hair and a stunning smile was striding toward them, his pretty green eyes flickering with the malice unique to the upper crust.

"Ferrin!" Captain Marcel of the city guard pushed Silver out of the way with a shoulder, gripping Ferrin's hand tight enough to make the bones grind together. He saw Ferrin's disgruntled look and turned to Silver, who was looking slightly dazed. "And isn't this that little fellow who fixes clothes? The one from Diabolos? Ah, Leonhart, you should've told me. I would have set you up with something a little more elevated than a bilge rat, eh?"

Ferrin stiffened. Bilge rat was a term nobles used for people from Diabolos when they were being viciously uncharitable. Even Wes, who fought pirates for a living, tensed when he heard people use the term. "He's nothing of the sort, Marcel."

"Well, can't blame you. Must be old habits, eh? Can't take the lower city out of the boy." Marcel laughed. "Still, he's pretty enough. Turn around, boy, show us your assets." He raised a hand, and Ferrin stepped between them, bristling.

"Speak like that again, and I'll—"

"I miss this, old boy." Marcel tapped Ferrin's chest, just a little too hard, the way he used to when he was "roughhousing" as a guard. "Catching up. I always forget what fun you are."

"Go sleep off the hangover, Marcel."

Marcel smiled. "I'm not nearly drunk enough to deal with whatever is going on here." He gestured at Ferrin, then looked at Silver and snorted. "Remarkable. This'll be a story to tell, Leonhart. What a family, eh? A spinster, a lump of ice—" he slapped Ferrin's chest again, "and the pretty one. What's his name? Wesley? Saw him at that award ceremony a year back; quite charming."

Ferrin felt his expression go still and cold. "We're done here, Marcel."

"Oh, sure. Used to be you'd be up in arms, little cub. The rat must've taught you some manners." He waved idly and turned away, leaving Ferrin like a stone on the expensive, gaudy rug.

"Hey." Silver touched his hand, and Ferrin realized he'd unthinkingly clenched it into a fist. "It's okay. He's just an asshole."

"I know that." Ferrin let out a long breath. "Thank you. He must be drunk—he doesn't usually throw it all out at once."

"Don't know how you worked with him without drowning him in a puddle somewhere, honestly," Silver said, and Ferrin laughed tightly. "But, um. While he was talking to you? I noticed something. There were nobles going into a little door by the bookshelf over there. They kept looking at the two of you."

Ferrin bit back a groan. Of course. Of *course*. "I shouldn't have let him distract me."

"Yeah, well, now we know he was a distraction, right?" Silver looped an arm through Ferrin's. "So maybe we go, uh, look at some books."

"Maybe we should." Ferrin let Silver tow him toward the bookshelf, eyeing Marcel from across the room. Marcel had cornered a woman, who was giggling softly, but he wasn't entirely sure if she wanted to be cornered in the first place. He tried to break away, and Silver gave him a look. A moment later, the woman had slipped away, and Marcel was opening another bottle of wine.

"He's a fucking menace," Ferrin whispered, and Silver patted his arm.

"I know. Really. Trust me." He reached for Ferrin's collar, and Ferrin looked down at him in surprise. "Kiss me, maybe? If we look like we're distracted, we can slip through that door without anyone thinking twice about it, yeah?"

Ferrin wondered if Silver wasn't trying for his own distraction, but he needed something nice to wash away the bitterness of having to see Marcel in the flesh. He cupped the back of Silver's neck and kissed him, too light. "I don't believe any of those things he said about you."

"Of course you don't," Silver said. "You're not a noble. You're a decent person."

Ferrin actually smiled and kissed Silver again. He backed him up toward the door, and Silver grabbed the lapels of his jacket, pulling him through and into a small, narrow hallway. It was unlit, but there was a door at the other end with a crack of light glowing at the bottom, broken by the occasional passing shadow.

"And this next one," someone was saying, as Silver closed the door after them, "is particularly fine. Note the flexibility, the craftsmanship."

"Look." Silver crouched at the edge of the hallway, sliding his hand along the wall. His voice was low, pitched so only Ferrin could hear him, and Ferrin could believe that he used to sneak around people's houses for a living. "There's another door next to this one. A panel."

"What? How do you know?"

"Rich people love that shit. It feels different when you're

looking for it." Silver did something with the wall, and a patch of darkness opened up next to the door. The space was very narrow, not enough for two people to pass comfortably, and they had to press together to squeeze inside.

Silver held a finger to his lips, and Ferrin nodded. They moved slowly, agonizingly slow until they reached the end of the hidden passage, where a grate was fixed into the wall. It was cleverly made so that someone could look out without being seen, but they had to push close together to both see through it, and they were left tangled, with Silver pinned under Ferrin with Ferrin half holding him against the wall. Ferrin gave Silver an apologetic look, and Silver grimaced.

"And the next one," someone said through the grate, and Ferrin leaned closer, adjusting his grip around Silver's waist. "All the way from exotic lands..."

The room was full of nobility. There were lords, ladies, and various gentry positioned everywhere in plush couches and ornate chairs, all facing a dais where Lord Rousseau stood. And on that dais, looking smug and wearing little more than a string around his waist, was...

"Gabriel from the House of Gold," Rousseau said with a flourish. "Our most distinguished courtesan of the auction, selling one exclusive night for five crowns."

* * *

The auction was for *people*.

No. Not just people. Submissives, and if Silver thought too much about that, he...well, thinking wasn't coming easy right now. Unlike Silver, who could come easy as anything if Ferrin would just—if he—

If I was up there, and he bid on me and took me to the—

"So, not a crown, then," Ferrin said softly, and his voice was soft and hot against Silver's ear, and the rest of Silver's thoughts flitted away into the middle distance.

Ferrin didn't say anything else, though, and for a moment, Silver wasn't sure if he was supposed to agree or what. He drew in a shuddery-sounding breath and made a motion with his head that was something like a nod. Or maybe he should have *not* nodded? Either way, there was no crown, just a lot of nobles eagerly bidding on the handsome young man smiling like a cat that ate the canary.

"Anyone in this room could hire him if they wanted," Ferrin continued as Silver died quietly of pent-up lust and a need to submit that was so strong that he would have been on his knees if Ferrin weren't holding him up. "There is no real need for this...spectacle."

There wasn't, but Silver found himself unable to stop thinking about the idea of it—being on display, being bid on, having someone want him enough to offer money in front of a crowd. And not just *someone*—Ferrin. Definitely Ferrin. And not just because he was currently pressed up against him in a space that was growing smaller by the second, despite how many laws of physics that very idea violated.

"It's—nobles," Silver managed, and why—why did Ferrin smell so good? Was that on purpose? Had he wanted to smell good for Silver? Or did everyone just get a whiff of his natural cologne and lose their mind, like Silver was doing *right now*?

"Yes," Ferrin said. And then, "Are you all right?"

Before Silver could answer, there was a raucous cheer from the crowd as the bidding for the pretty courtesan came to a conclusion. Silver, who was pressed up against Ferrin, couldn't see—and honestly, he didn't much care since he was dying from the feel of Ferrin's strong body pressed up against his own.

"Sure," he managed weakly. "Great. What's happening?"

"Oh." Ferrin cleared his throat softly. "The, ah. Winner of

the auction—Lady Bellerive, I believe—is, ah. Making him kneel, there, on the stage."

Silver drew in a breath, but before he could say anything, Ferrin went still and murmured, "Be quiet," which Silver thought meant someone was coming near their hiding place.

He didn't bother pointing out that he hadn't been talking. Because Ferrin slid a hand down to his waist and pulled him in even tighter, and honestly, there could be a royal symphony playing in the room beyond, and Silver wouldn't have noticed it.

That's it, this is where I die, he thought miserably, pressed up against the full length of Ferrin's impossibly gorgeous body.

That wasn't the worst thing, though—actually, it was the *best* thing—because his body was reacting without his permission, and his cock was so hard he was sure that if Ferrin couldn't feel it, the man would have to be dead.

He definitely felt it. Ferrin didn't say anything, but the fingers on the back of Silver's waist tightened slightly, and as close as they were, Silver could feel more than hear his soft inhale.

"It's fine," Ferrin whispered.

"I can't breathe," Silver whispered back. He closed his eyes in mortification. "You're very. Tall."

A huff again, this time of a laugh. "Don't worry. It's flattering. But you *do* need to breathe."

That was easier said than done, especially given the sounds coming from the room behind them. There was someone— someone was being *flogged,* and Silver wasn't one for pain, but the sounds were intoxicating, and the thought of being tied up and restrained, being shown off—it wasn't helping his situation in the slightest.

Now he couldn't breathe *or* stand still, and his entire body felt like it was on fire from the combination of so much hot captain of the guard against him and the sounds of dominants taking their pleasure in submissives. Silver needed to—he couldn't—he—

He felt Ferrin shift, his hand sliding around to press against the ridge of Silver's cock through his pants, and if that wasn't enough, he murmured, "Shh, I'll settle you," and that was pretty much it for Silver.

Ferrin managed to get his pants unbuttoned, and Silver pressed his burning-hot face into Ferrin's chest as Ferrin's callused fingers curled around his throbbing erection. He started stroking, and Silver's legs began to immediately shake as pleasure washed over him, so intense it made him bite his own lip to hold back a moan.

"That's it," Ferrin urged, and the confines of their hiding place filled with the sound of Silver's breathing and muffled attempts to keep his moans quiet. Which honestly, why was he bothering? It wasn't like anyone would notice a few more moans added with the rest.

Ferrin shifted again, and after the second of panic that he was going to *stop*, Silver realized it was so that Ferrin could stroke him *and* press his own erection against Silver's. Silver wanted to say something like, *the spectacle getting to you, too, huh?* but it came out as a whine and a wish he could bite Ferrin's strong pecs through his clothes.

"Stay quiet and take it for me, good *boy*," Ferrin breathed, and Silver's knees buckled. The dark chuckle that drew from Ferrin almost had him come right then and there, and Silver both wanted to and didn't because that meant it would be over.

"Could you—against the wall, please," Silver managed because while his cock loved the attention, his submission needed just a little more. Luckily, Ferrin understood and moved them both without stopping the delicious stroke of his hand on Silver's cock, and moved so he could press Silver against the wall.

That was great, perfect, and it also meant that now Silver could see what was happening—submissives kneeling, sucking off party guests, the lucky lady who'd won the auction for Gabriel sprawled on a chaise with one hand in his hair and his head between her spread thighs—and his eyes locked on a beautiful courtesan in shibari, kneeling and staring up adoringly at a noble who was checking over the ropes and rubbing a thumb over the submissive's lower lip while he reached for the fastening of his pants.

Orgies had never been Silver's fantasy, but like hell he wasn't getting ideas from the rope bondage and the praise he could hear filtering through to their cramped hiding place.

Ferrin took Silver's chin in his fingers, bringing his gaze up, and even in the muted light, Silver could see the intense look in Ferrin's gorgeous dark eyes. "Look at me, not them."

Silver blinked, tried to nod, and moaned instead when Ferrin's hand twisted over the top of his cock. He was trembling, and Ferrin's dominance was fairly bleeding from him, and the sounds and sights of the debaucherous ongoings faded until there was nothing left but the handsome dominant bringing him off.

"You're so fucking hot," Silver whispered, bucking slightly into his hand, and—oh, fuck, *yes,* Ferrin inched closer to keep him *still,* which made him whimper.

Ferrin didn't smile, but he leaned in and kissed him, possessive and rough, his hand gliding easily since Silver's cock was already wet. "That's it, good. You're going to come for me."

"Literally—anytime—" Silver panted, wriggling only so he could raise his arms and put them above his head, crossed at the wrists, tilting his head as much as he could to bare his throat.

Ferrin swore softly and bit him, firm but not hard, enough pain to ease the aching need to submit as he ground his erection against Silver's hip. "Tell me one thing you're watching that's getting you so hard."

"You," Silver said immediately.

He could feel Ferrin smile against his neck. "Besides me."

Gods, that *voice*, rough and low, was driving him wild. "The —shibari."

"That is what you'd like, isn't it? To be still." Ferrin rubbed his fingers over Silver's balls, and Silver's eyes crossed as he felt himself near the edge. "What color for you, then? Blue? Red? Black?"

"I—please, sir," Silver babbled, unable to answer as he was so close he couldn't think what any of those words even *meant*.

"Answer the question, or you won't come," Ferrin threatened.

Silver had to think about it, drawing in as much of a breath as he could before he disobeyed and came all over Ferrin's ridiculously wonderful, perfect hand. As long as Ferrin was the one tying him up, Silver could give fuck-all what color the ropes were. But he wanted to come, and more than that, he wanted to *obey*.

"Blue," he managed, finally. "Blue ropes. Sir. Sir, please— I'm so close—"

"You are, aren't you?" Ferrin's voice had a wicked bent, one Silver had never heard before but honestly wanted to hear for the rest of his life, forever, in lieu of literally anything else. "Blue to match your eyes, pretty thing?"

"Match—your uniform," Silver gasped, banging his head back against the wall, and oh, fuck, he was going to come *right now*; he needed to, wanted to so badly.

Ferrin went momentarily still, but before Silver could beg again, he made a low, rough sound like a growl and ground his hard cock against Silver's hip. He put his mouth right against Silver's ear and said, "Now you may come, pretty boy."

Silver barely lasted until the words were out before he came, with Ferrin kissing the desperate, relieved gasps spilling from his mouth as he shook with pleasure. Ferrin stroked him until the last pulse faded, and Silver grabbed him when he moved back, tangling his fingers in Ferrin's coat and gulping in air.

Ferrin tipped his chin up, stared into Silver's face—which felt flushed and hot and damp with sweat—and said quietly, "Kneel."

Silver hit the ground so fast it sent a shock of pain up through his legs, and he didn't care about it one little bit. Kneeling felt so good, almost as much as the orgasm, and pressed his face against Ferrin's thigh while Ferrin petted his hair and murmured, *Good boy. You did so well. Breathe for me. Settle,* over and over again.

As he calmed, Silver turned his head slightly...and he could just make out the shape of Ferrin's cock under his fine trousers. He wasn't even aware enough to ask first, just moved enough to rub his face against him, mouth immediately watering at how badly he wanted it in his mouth.

"Please, sir," Silver whispered and thrilled at the slight groan that earned, his breath on Ferrin's cock. "Let me?"

A heartbeat, and then Ferrin breathed out a, "yes, go on," and Silver reached eagerly for his belt, already excited at the idea of letting Ferrin fuck his mouth, choke him with that impressive cock of his until he cried, coming all over Silver's face...

When there was a click, a sound, and a sudden *woosh* of air...followed by a lot more light than there should be.

And the odious, completely unwanted sound of Captain Marcel's voice drawling, "Well, well. Here it seems our Captain Ferrin isn't as straightlaced as we thought."

It looked like the party was over.

Chapter Six

Ferrin emerged from the secret alcove to a round of applause.

Someone like Marcel would have brushed it off. He would have turned it into a grand joke, one he certainly knew about well ahead of time, and would be having drinks and sharing his exploits by the end of the night. Ferrin didn't have Marcel's so-called natural charm, however. He stood there, a hand around Silver's arm, his clothes rumpled, and gave Marcel a cold look.

"Considering you partook in a courtesan auction without the Pleasure District's patronage and took efforts to withhold it from me, I believe we are on even footing, Marcel."

"We just wanted to see if we could, really," Rousseau said before he was hushed into silence.

Marcel grinned, a hand on the hilt of his sword like a rank amateur, and reached out to touch Silver's chin. Silver jerked away, and Ferrin stepped between them.

"That's hardly fair," Marcel said. "You should let someone else have a turn, Captain. The poor man looks woefully underwhelmed, and it isn't as though you paid much for him."

"He isn't a courtesan," Ferrin said, and when Marcel raised his brows, he added, "or a whore. Let us through. I've seen enough."

"I'm sure you have." Ferrin started off down the dark hallway, pulling Silver after him, and Marcel's voice drifted in a sing-song at his back. "I'm sure you needed to let off steam after that trouble at the palace."

Ferrin stopped. When he turned, he saw Marcel framed by the light of the auction room, hand still on his hilt, swaying slightly on his feet. "What was that?"

"You know. The trouble." Marcel tapped his brow. "Shame, isn't it if the captain of the guard can't even manage such a basic task?"

Ferrin could hear Silver take a sharp breath behind him. Rumor was an insidious thing in the palace, but the king would not have told a guard captain with a fondness for drink and a tendency to sell his secrets at a thought. If the truth had gotten to Marcel, the man would be on unofficial house arrest, not drinking himself to a stupor at a courtesan auction.

"Yes," Ferrin said carefully. "A shame. I heard you were in the palace that day, Marcel. Ordering my guards about."

"Well, someone has to. Imagine Captain Ferrin, upright Captain *Ferrin,* letting someone walk off with the—"

"Let's go," Silver said quickly, his voice echoing in the narrow hallway. He laid a hand on Ferrin's chest. "I don't really want to hear what a man with a broken dick has to say, anyway."

Ferrin stared down at him, and Silver winked as Marcel, watched by the entire room at his back, sputtered and started forward.

"What did that gutter rat say?"

"You think it ain't obvious?" Silver's voice slid easily into the cant of the thieves in the guild, matching their cadence and light tone almost perfectly. "Anyone who's anyone in the palace knows old Marcel can't keep it up more than a minute. The maidservants have a game, you see, of who can get through an hour with poor Marcy without falling asleep in the middle. Ain't nothing wrong with it, but it's a pain when he keeps trying to press a suit that won't rise if you know what I mean."

Ferrin raised his brows. "Having some trouble, Marcel?"

"I have a friend who makes powder for that," a noble said from the room behind him, and Marcel stepped forward, reaching for Silver. When Silver sidestepped him, he raised his hand and closed his palm into a fist.

Ferrin, seeing no other recourse, promptly slapped him.

There was a rush of whispers through the door, and Marcel fell back, snarling, as Ferrin adjusted his cuffs. "You don't raise a hand to a member of the palace staff, Marcel. I'll have satisfaction from you to the blood by tomorrow at noon."

"At sunset," Marcel spat. "In the training yards. As the challenged, I pick the time."

"And as the challenger, I state the terms. Your captaincy, Marcel. When I draw blood, you'll turn in your badge and submit yourself to the crown for questioning."

Marcel barked out a laugh. "You can't be serious."

"Are you rejecting a challenge?" Ferrin glanced at the nobles and courtesans through the door to the auction room. If Marcel backed out now, he'd be a disgrace in noble circles within the hour, and Marcel knew it. He rubbed his cheek and glowered in Ferrin's direction, still swaying.

"And if you lose, you turn the palace guard to me."

That, Ferrin knew, would never happen. Emile would simply hand it over, smile blandly, and then hand it right back. "Very well."

"No." A glint of malicious, small-minded evil shone in

Marcel's eyes. "No, it won't be that easy. You lose, and you don't say a word." Ferrin knit his brows, and Marcel smiled, lowering his voice so the others couldn't hear. "Not when I send guards to your sister's place for an inspection. Not when I pull a favor with my friends in the navy. Not when I pay this one triple what you offered. Not a word, Ferrin."

Ferrin considered how many words he could conceivably say while running Marcel through and nodded. "Silence, then."

"Fucking idiot," Marcel said, pushing past him. "Remember who won in the practice yards, Captain."

Ferrin said nothing, letting the door to the hallway slam shut behind him, and ran a hand through his hair.

"Well," Silver said in a faint voice. "No one ever dueled for my honor before."

"You have more honor than he does," Ferrin said, taking Silver by the arm again. "Let's go before the crowd descends."

They barely made it. There was a gaggle of nobles at their heels when they made it to the front door, clamoring for attention, but all Ferrin wanted to do was go home, put Silver on his knees, and pretend the rest of the evening hadn't happened.

"Do you think..." Silver struggled to keep up, grasping Ferrin's hand. "Do you think he'll really threaten your siblings?"

"Pretty sure he crossed that line," Ferrin said, passing the line of carriages.

"But he won't win," Silver said carefully. Ferrin looked down at him, surprised to find Silver's eyes were bright with worry, his teeth scraping over his lower lip.

"Oh. No. Not at all. That man hasn't touched a sword to do more than wave it about for a crowd in years."

"But he said...in the training yards."

"Yes, when we were recruits, he did beat me. But my sword was unbalanced. This is an official challenge, on my own ground." Still, Marcel had been formidable when they were young. There was a chance a spark of that raw talent was still there, hidden beneath years of neglect.

"He shouldn't have raised a hand to you," he added, and Silver looked down. "And you heard what he said. He knows what was stolen. What I want to know is why. If we can get him to Isiodore and Sabre for questioning, we may be a step closer to fixing this mess."

"And him turning in his badge?"

Ferrin flashed Silver a small, private smile. "That was for me."

Silver locked his hands behind his back, and Ferrin realized, a little too late, that he was still half dragging him down the street. He let go, and Silver shot him a sidelong look. "I'm not saying I mind being manhandled."

Ferrin led them down the dark, winding streets to his neighborhood, letting the high buildings of the Starian elite pass them by. "If you'd like, we can always... my house is open."

"You mean do I want to suck your cock until I choke on it?" Silver asked, and Ferrin let out a startled laugh. Silver grinned. "I mean, you just challenged someone for my honor. Isn't that the rules?"

"Ain't noble, Silver; the rules don't apply to me."

"Okay, then let's make up new ones. Getting a duel of honor in your name means you need to kneel. It'll be like protocol."

Ferrin looked out over the quiet street, with its tidy little buildings and carefully-sculpted gardens. "I tend to prefer that. Protocol."

"Oh. Like... kneeling a certain way?"

Ferrin kept his gaze fixed on the street. "Or other things. Not using the furniture without permission. Occasional voice restrictions. The way they walk or address me in public and private. Rules for dress."

Silver was silent for a moment. Ferrin knew not every

submissive enjoyed the level of protocol Ferrin's dominance required. It was intense—overwhelming. Someone who thought they wouldn't mind it ended up discovering that it felt too demeaning or too vulnerable, and it would lead to a messy drop and an awkward conversation before parting ways.

"Okay," Silver said at last. "Hot."

Ferrin looked at him. Silver's face was flushed, and he still had his hands behind his back, twisting his wrist in one hand. "You say that now. But there should be limitations—you can't expect to follow them all the time."

"How would you like me to walk?" Silver asked, all innocence. Ferrin faltered, and Silver came to a halt, head slightly tilted. "Sir?"

Ferrin reminded himself, through the rush of dominance threatening to overtake him, that he couldn't just push Silver up against the nearest fence and fuck his mouth. The neighbors would complain. Still, it was a near thing, with Silver looking up at him with earnest patience, hands behind his back.

"A step behind," Ferrin said. "Don't look me in the eyes without permission." Silver fell into step perfectly, without question, and Ferrin suppressed a shiver. "You're sure."

"Yes, sir." Silver smiled just a little, and Ferrin had to force himself to walk the rest of the way to his house. When they reached the door, Silver waited for Ferrin to enter first and knelt without asking to help remove his boots. Ferrin took a sharp breath, staring down at Silver with his head bowed in his fine clothes, kneeling for him in his darkened home.

"Is there something you'd like me to—"

"We'll discuss that later," Ferrin said, a little too sharply, and Silver took a breath, sitting back up on his knees. "Right now, I need you naked, at the foot of my bed, on your knees."

"Yes, sir," Silver said, and before Ferrin could even think to give the order, he got to his hands and knees.

* * *

Ferrin had *challenged someone for him.*

If he lived to be a thousand, Silver would never get over it. He wasn't the kind of man you challenged someone over. He was the sort of man you ignored or smiled at without meaning it. Hell, he could barely get nobles to *stand still* to take their measurements! He wasn't all that offended at *gutter rat*, either—honestly, gutter rats knew when to run and how to survive, and honestly, that mix of determination and intuition...well, he doubted Captain Marcel would thrive as well as the rats, with all his power taken away, forced to live out of sight and survive on scraps.

But he didn't want to think about that odious man right now. He was on his hands and knees, crawling after a handsome dominant, and that was enough to soothe the chaos of his mind for the moment. He liked that Ferrin was into protocol and orders, rules and stipulations. It meant Silver wouldn't disappoint him because Ferrin would make sure that Silver acted exactly as he wanted.

The relief of it was...overwhelming. Silver was used to indulging his submission through service and an occasional spanking or kneeling to suck cock, but he'd never had someone take such *care* of him before. He loved the idea that Ferrin could express exactly what he wanted in clear, certain terms, and Silver just had to follow the instructions, which he was more than willing to do.

By the time he got to the bedroom, his cock was already hard again, as if he'd not gotten off in the hidden passage only an hour or so ago. Ferrin was standing by the window, shoulders straight, gaze sharp as he watched Silver.

Silver paused, on his hands and knees, and knelt—just as he had earlier, feeling the satisfaction of it settle him, ground him.

He spoke to Ferrin, posture straight, but kept his gaze lowered. "May I stand, Sir? You wanted me naked."

"Yes, you may."

Silver got to his feet and started stripping. He wasn't a brat by any means, but the urge to toss his clothes to the floor just to see what Ferrin would do was overwhelming. He paused and heard Ferrin say quietly, "I don't care to be tested, put those away properly," and it turned out that being sexily reminded was even better than being sexily reprimanded.

"You may fold the pants and the shirt and put them on the dresser, there," Ferrin continued, and his dominance felt different now than it had at the party. There it felt like a sword, edged and deadly. Here was more like...a firm hand, or soft cuffs. Something weighted, not gentle, but *inescapable.*

He's like leather and iron and oak. Strong, hearty, faithful, and unbending. Silver let the thought come and go, as now wasn't the time to think about elements or how good Ferrin would look in black, silver, and green. Ferrin would look good in anything. Right now, Silver was supposed to be in *nothing*, so he better get to it. He put the clothes on the dresser and then hung up his coat as instructed, everything orderly.

Silver went and knelt again at the foot of Ferrin's bed. His breath caught when he saw Ferrin holding a pair of cuffs, which were indeed leather with soft fur lining the insides, and his wrists twitched in anticipation of feeling them there.

"Do you want these?" Ferrin held them up.

"Yes, Sir," he breathed, swallowing hard, keeping his wrists crossed, his shoulders back. He kept his chin up, too, because... well, he felt pretty damn proud of himself at the moment. He was kneeling for the hottest dominant in Duciel, Staria, *maybe* all of Iperios, and that dominant had issued a *challenge* in his *honor.* Who wouldn't be proud to kneel for a dominant like that?

He did, however, keep his gaze lowered as he figured Ferrin would appreciate it. Ferrin made a pleased sound and touched his shoulders, gently eased Silver's knees a bit farther apart with his foot, and then tilted his face up with his fingers under Silver's chin. "Look at me. There you go. What puts you under?"

Silver blinked. His cock was hard already, and he could feel himself starting to slip under, that curious, dizzy sensation that felt like sliding into a warm bath on a cold day. "This, Sir. You, ah. Making me please you, just right. Following instructions."

"Which means you also like the praise, hmm?" Ferrin smiled down at him. "Well? I asked you a question."

Ah, fuck. Of course, he liked praise. Were there people who didn't? But it felt...admitting it, well, that felt a little needy. Desperate. And Silver both hated and loved that feeling because wanting something always made you vulnerable. Asking for something meant someone could reject you.

He tried nodding, but Ferrin just clicked his tongue and shook his head, a smile fading. "No," he said sharply, and Silver winced, feeling the sting of that disapproval like a slap. "Answer me out loud. Yes, sir, or no, sir."

"Yes, Sir," Silver admitted, blushing. "I do like it."

"Why does that embarrass you?"

Well, okay, so it seemed like Ferrin was into sexy interrogations, which Silver would have said was not his thing, except for how his body was reacting like it very much *was*. "I don't like to...ask for things I don't deserve. Sir," he added quickly when Ferrin's fingers tightened on his chin.

"You think you don't deserve to know when you're doing well?" Ferrin asked and clicked again. "I didn't tell you to look away."

"I think I don't do well enough, um, Sir," Silver said softly, and he knew that sounded a bit nonsensical, so he tried to clarify. "I don't think I've earned it. Praise."

"You earn it if I say you do," Ferrin told him. "Do you understand that, Silver? I don't give praise that isn't earned. So if I praise you, then you've earned it."

"I—I understand, Sir."

"Ah." Ferrin nodded and dropped his hand from Silver's chin. "Maybe you don't. But you will."

Well, that was hot enough that Silver almost combusted right there. He wasn't given instructions, so he didn't do anything but kneel there, holding form with a raging erection and his breath coming too fast. All the while, Ferrin continued to make slight alterations to his form that seemed, to Silver anyway, to be thinly-veiled excuses to touch him. But it ended with him putting the cuffs around Silver's wrists, so that was just fine.

When Ferrin came back around to the front, his hand went to his belt buckle, and Silver only just resisted the urge to lean forward and try and help him out. He wasn't entirely sure if he'd ever unbuttoned or unzipped someone's pants with his teeth before, but he was more than willing to give it a try.

Ferrin didn't tell him to, though, so Silver just stared hungrily, still breathing a little too loudly as Ferrin freed his cock.

"I'll make sure you suck it just like I want you to," Ferrin assured him in a husky voice as he lightly smacked the side of Silver's face with his cock, which, if anything, almost made him fall over out of sheer hotness and surprise... "So when I praise you, you won't argue with me."

"N—no, sir. I won't argue," Silver promised, practically babbling before Ferrin took his hair in one hand and guided his cock in Silver's mouth with the other.

"Tip your head back—ah, there, rub your tongue on the

bottom, that's it," Ferrin praised, and Silver's entire body went liquid-hot as Ferrin continued to use his crisp, official guard captain's voice to give Silver the dirtiest blowjob instructions in the world. "Suck on the head of my cock, that's it, good, use your tongue, let me fuck your throat—"

Silver was, at one point, squirming on his knees from being so overwhelmed, both by Ferrin's dominance and perfect control—the hand in Silver's hair never pulled, not once, merely held him and moved him about as he wanted—and Ferrin merely pulled his cock free and said quietly, "Settle, now," and Silver did.

Silver had been under before—he actually had a fairly easy time with that, which wasn't always a boon given he'd spent his life around self-important nobles, whether as a tailor *or* a thief— and he'd even been put under by sucking cock. But that involved a bit more manhandling, or maybe rougher treatment was a better word since Silver didn't mind it. But Ferrin, all it took was that firm grip on his hair and his filthy mouth issuing commands, and Silver knew he'd be under sooner rather than later.

Ferrin eased his cock in deeper, his free hand lightly tipping Silver's chin back and then stroking over his throat. Silver moaned around Ferrin's cock, blinking up at him, feeling himself start to choke a bit but not moving away. He felt his muscles aching at holding position and forced himself to stay still, to be used.

"Keep your shoulders straight, eyes on me while I fuck your mouth," Ferrin said, and honestly, Silver would do whatever he wanted, forever, if he just used that *voice* all the time. How was half the royal guard not in love with him? Maybe they were.

And he'd chosen Silver.

"That's it, ah, good," Ferrin praised when Silver let the feeling of pride wash over him, gaze steady on Ferrin's. "See?

You're more than earning your praise, boy. Taking my cock so well."

Silver moaned again, and Ferrin went deep enough that he choked again but didn't fight, didn't struggle...and didn't let himself slump or shift. Instead, he kept his posture perfect while still remaining pliant, allowing Ferrin to do as he wanted. Giving himself over to a dominant who took control with simple touches and that low, pleased voice.

It was a messy blowjob, for all Silver was trying to be still and composed, and he realized hazily after a bit that must be what Ferrin wanted—a submissive falling to pieces, but *properly*, under Ferrin's hand. His own cock felt like a rock and so sensitive that it throbbed when the air in the room shifted around them.

"I think you've earned it on your pretty face," Ferrin said in a warm voice, and Silver thought he could probably get off just fine every day for the rest of his life, thinking about that.

But he said nothing, just let Ferrin pull his head back with a gentle tug on his hair, then panted up Ferrin, blinking owlishly as Ferrin worked his hand over himself, keeping Silver right where he wanted him.

Silver might have opened his mouth, done something... sexy...but he was under and hadn't been given instructions, so he simply knelt there and kept his face turned up, breathing eventually settling as he watched Ferrin's hand twist over the head of his slick, wet cock. He came with a soft moan, and Silver kept his eyes open as long as he could, sighing in quiet satisfaction as Ferrin finished.

He was dimly aware of Ferrin dragging his fingers through the mess on his face and opened his mouth obediently when Ferrin tapped the side of his face. He licked and sucked Ferrin's fingers clean, smiling at nothing in particular and trying not to fall face-forward on the floor. He loved this, being put under by someone who knew what they were doing, whose dominance was such a strong match for his own tendencies. Silver felt Ferrin touch his shoulder and heard his murmur that he was undoing the cuffs, and then Ferrin gently helped him to his feet. He let himself go where he was led and blinked in surprise when he realized he was staring at...himself?

Himself, naked and flushed, with messy hair and a flushed face, wet mouth, and hard cock. And Ferrin, standing behind him in the mirror, still dressed in everything but his coat and boots, his hands on either side of Silver's arms.

"Different isn't it," Ferrin murmured, leaning down to kiss the side of Silver's neck. "When you're the one standing in front of the mirror?"

Silver stood in front of mirrors all the time, but he knew what Ferrin meant. He nodded, forcing himself to say, "Yes, sir," in a soft voice.

"The difference, of course, is that you don't need fine clothes to be beautiful. Look at you." Ferrin's touched his face, lightly turning Silver's face back toward the full-length mirror. "You're gorgeous. Under, mess, your cock hard. For me, isn't it? All of it? Tell me it is."

"Yes, sir," Silver said because that was easy to admit, even if it was still so hard to speak. He also couldn't meet Ferrin's gaze for longer than a second. Being under was always nice, but this was—intense. It made him wonder if he'd ever really done it fully the way you were supposed to. Maybe all those other times, he was on the edge without going under.

"Sometime, I'm going to fuck you like this," Ferrin continued, proving that he was, possibly, the hottest person ever to draw breath on the planet. "Make you watch yourself. You should see how you look when you go under. You did it just as I wanted."

Silver felt his eyes go hot, and in the mirror, he could see them get bright and watery. He was shaking a bit, and yeah, this was...instead of coming back up or getting his wits back, he felt like he was going deeper the longer Ferrin stood there behind him, steady and strong.

"It's all right," Ferrin murmured, hands on his shoulder. "You don't have to meet my eyes, and you don't have to speak. Voice-and-gaze restrictions, nod, so I know you understand."

He nodded, and the relief was...delicious, pushing him down more, and the lovely, beautiful quiet in his mind felt like floating on a calm, warm sea on his back like he used to do on lazy summer days as a kid back in Diabolos. But then came a sudden bolt of pleasure, and he realized he'd half-closed his eyes and wasn't paying attention to Ferrin...who was still there, one hand on Silver's hip and the other stroking Silver's cock with... something soft?

He blinked, staring at Ferrin's hand, remembering he wasn't supposed to look or ask questions. And the more he concentrated on himself in the mirror, being stroked off by Ferrin so tall and gorgeous behind him...he found he didn't much care.

"You don't have to be still; you can move. Don't speak, but you can make noise. Do you know what this is? Have you figured it out?" Ferrin's laugh was low and wicked, and it made Silver shiver—then moan in frustration as Ferrin stopped moving at all. "The scrap of velvet from your shop. I put it in my pocket. Feels good, doesn't it? Do you want to know how I know? You can nod."

Silver nodded frantically, and since he was allowed to move...he tried to fuck Ferrin's hand and was delighted when Ferrin let him.

"I did this. To myself. To see how it would feel, and because I wanted to think about you."

Silver squeezed his eyes shut, aware of his own loud breathing, and suddenly realized how close he was to the edge. His toes curled, his calves went tense, and when Ferrin told him to open his eyes, he did so with considerable effort.

"I like watching you fuck my hand like this," Ferrin said, and Silver decided that meant *do it more*, so he did, realizing his hands weren't cuffed and that he was digging his fingers into his own thighs to keep from coming without permission. "No, don't. If you need to grab something, grab me."

Silver was momentarily torn between not wanting to come without permission and also wanting to touch Ferrin however he was allowed...then he remembered it wasn't up to him. The relief of not having to choose was nice, so he reached back and grabbed at Ferrin's trousers, even if it didn't ground him quite as well as it had when he was digging his nails into his own skin.

"Do you like thinking about that, me stroking myself, thinking about you?" Ferrin moved his hand, too, so now Silver was chasing the movement, desperate, sweaty, and crying with a mix of frustration and submission.

He couldn't speak, so he nodded a little wildly—and then started to panic, wondering how he was going to ask to come and if he couldn't ask, did that mean he couldn't come? Because then he would die, and that wouldn't be very good for anyone.

"I know what you want," Ferrin said, hand firm on his hip, the other hand stroking him faster, the velvet scrap sliding smoothly up and down Silver's hard shaft. "Be still. That's it. Don't close your eyes, watch—watch yourself—"

Silver had never watched himself like this before, and it was...strange to see himself falling apart like this, absolutely stripped of all control. The floaty feeling returned again, and he didn't fight it, let himself shake there and moan, and bit his own lip to keep from begging because he was still under voice restrictions. He couldn't speak, couldn't even look pleadingly at Ferrin, could just stand there and watch his own knees shake in the reflection, feel his balls tighten, and watch how wet his cock was growing in the mirror.

"You can be off voice restrictions as long as you use your voice to beg for it, prettily and properly," Ferrin instructed, and he was so warm, a constant, strong presence at Silver's back. Giving him strength and stability, even as he stripped it all away.

"Please," Silver managed. "Please, sir."

"Please, sir, what?" Ferrin asked, fingers curling loosely, too loosely, around Silver's cock.

Please let me come, is what Silver meant to say. What he wanted to say, because of course he wanted to come, was so close to it....

"Please let me close my eyes," is what he said.

Ferrin paused, just for a moment, and then said, "No. You look beautiful. You're doing so well; you should see. You earned it. Tell me you earned it."

"I—" Silver bit his lip, wondering why this was harder than any of it.

"Say you earned it, and you may come," Ferrin ordered, dominance filtering through his words. "Don't, and I'll edge you until you're sobbing. You know which one I want."

Okay, but they were going to have to put a pin in that *edge you until you're sobbing* thing because that...wouldn't be bad. Silver dragged in a breath, squirmed a bit, and said softly, "I earned it, Sir. Please let me come."

"Yes," Ferrin said. "Look at me, and yes. You may."

Silver only barely managed to drag his gaze up to Ferrin's, before he came all over Ferrin's hand and the scrap of velvet. It was hard to keep his eyes open, but he did for as long as he could, and before the rush of his pleasure overtook him and forced his eyes closed...he could see Ferrin's pleased, proud smile in the mirror.

Ferrin insisted on cleaning him up, bringing him water, and then putting the cuffs back on—albeit in front, this time, and not clipped together—just so he could settle. He let Silver lay on his back on the bed, hands up and comfortably crossed at the wrists, thinking if this was really the first time he'd ever been under properly...he wasn't sure he ever wanted to come back up.

Chapter Seven

For the first time since he'd earned his badge as a captain, Ferrin woke after sunrise.

It was still early, with just a sliver of light spilling over the bed from the narrow window, but it still felt decadent, selfish, a private moment stolen away. Ferrin turned and found Silver curled up at his side, hair messy, looking up at him with the air of a man half awake.

"You have more freckles than I thought," Ferrin said, momentarily robbed of his senses with the knowledge of Silver's hand on his hip and his gaze soft and welcoming. He really did have a wealth of freckles, fading ones hidden behind darker spots, like shadows. Only someone who came close would be able to tell.

"And you're fucking gorgeous," Silver said, smiling. "I want to make you breakfast."

Ferrin laughed softly and kissed Silver's cheek. Then his neck, then his collarbone, until Silver was suddenly quite awake and gasping beneath him, hands skimming up Ferrin's shoulders. He hadn't indulged his dominance in years, not so fully, and he was still buzzing with it, savoring the way Silver seemed to know exactly what to do to rouse him, the way he tossed his head or flexed his fingers. Ferrin grabbed Silver by the hips, thumbs brushing close to his already hardening cock, and Silver whispered a curse that made Ferrin bare his teeth in a smile.

Then, to his utter horror, he heard his sister's voice.

"This ain't a break-in!" A door slammed in the distance, and Silver cursed louder and burrowed under the sheets as Ferrin rolled over him to pick up their clothes. At least they were folded—yet another perk of following protocol—but he'd only managed to shove Silver's under the sheets when he heard footsteps thumping across the room outside.

"Does your sister have a key?" Silver whispered, moving about under the covers while Ferrin put on trousers.

"For emergencies," Ferrin said, raising his voice. "She has a key for *emergencies.*"

"Pretty sure gettin' your heart bled out by the captain of the city guard is a bleeding emergency, you fecking—" Louise swung open the bedroom door, staring numbly at the lump that was Silver on the bed. "Who're you talking to?"

"Have you heard of knocking, Lou?"

Louise whirled on him, shock replaced by pure anger. It took a bit for her lower city accent to come back, but it was there in full force, making her sound just like their father. "Don't Lou me, don't you dare Lou me. I'll tell Mam about this duel of yours, and she'll tell Wes."

"That's underhanded, Lou."

"Is Wes more frightening than your parents?" Silver asked, popping his head out from under the sheets. "Hello, Louise. How's Armand and the kids?"

Louise blinked. "Outside, eating cake. Ferrin, is this the man you challenged Marcel to a duel over? It's everywhere on the street right now. The baker across from me sent one of her little messenger boys with a note."

"Don't think you should talk to that baker," Ferrin started to say, but Louise was only just getting started.

"I appreciate that you seem to have found yourself a man—and you're very nice, Silver—"

"Thanks," Silver said, buttoning his shirt.

"—but Marcel has wanted to gut you nose to navel since that *bastard* ran off after he *beat* you, and he won't play pretty and polite like you do. He's a rich boy, Ferrie; you know what rich boys are."

"Ferrie?" Silver asked, smiling slightly.

"He raised a hand to Silver," Ferrin said, his voice clipped. "What would you have done, Lou?"

Louise stood there, fuming silently, before finally looking away. "Fine. I would have stabbed him."

"And you would have done it without needing romantic entanglements," Ferrin added, not looking at Silver. Louise rolled her eyes.

"I know." She glanced over at Silver and smiled sidelong. "People say my brother's the unfeeling one, but I'm the one who doesn't fall in love."

"Except you'd fight the king himself for a possum you found in the garbage, so everyone thinks you're a romantic anyway."

"Yes, it's a curse." Louise tossed her braids over a shoulder. "Wait. You're distracting me."

Damn.

"You tried," Silver whispered, getting out of bed, mostly dressed. "But I don't think Marcel can beat him, Louise. He's a drunk and a coward."

"Drunks can get lucky, and cowards want to live," Louise snapped. "Where is it? When? I'll need to be there if I'm your second."

"My...Louise. No. It isn't even to the death."

Louise glared him down. "Where and when."

Ferrin sighed. Louise had been enrolled in the same lessons when they were young—she had every right to request to be Ferrin's second. "Sunset, in the training yards by the barracks."

"Good. I'll be there. He must like you," she added, looking at Silver. "He's right—I'd do it for anyone. But Ferrin has to really feel it to lose his temper over a person." She straightened her shoulders. "I hope you've fixed that trouble with your right side."

"I haven't left my side open since we were fifteen, Lou."

Louise shrugged. "So you say. But be prepared. Everyone knows now. You'll have a crowd come sunset."

Ferrin nodded, wanting nothing more than to ensure his sister was out of his house and unable to start asking questions about why Silver was in his bed when it struck him that she was right. There would be people there—including anyone who may have told Marcel about the theft of the crown, wanting to ensure that he didn't point an accusatory finger their way. He grinned, and Louise drew back, suspicion in every line of her face.

"You are, as always, a marvel," Ferrin said and kissed her forehead. Louise sputtered.

"Yes, I know, but you'd better not be up to something, Ferrin. That's the same look you had when we used to sneak into the candy cabinet."

Silver, who was leaning against the doorway, beamed.

"I'll tell you later, Louise. When it isn't confidential."

"Oh, like how the boy who stole something from the palace is confidential?" Louise raised her hands in the air, backing into the living room. "Since you're here, Silver, Armand wants to talk to you. He won't tell me what's troubling him, but he says you'd get it, whatever that means."

Silver's smile faded. "Does he want to talk now?"

"I'll bring him by tomorrow when this nonsense is over. And

no, Ferrin, they won't be watching. I'm not traumatizing children today, thank you."

"Your brother, though, that's just fine."

Louise's eyes twinkled. "You're a big boy. You can handle it."

Ferrin pointed her out the door, and Louise opened it, revealing Armand and his siblings trying to shove their ears to the door.

"Is he gonna die?" Armand asked as the door shut at last. Ferrin covered his face with a hand.

"Candy cabinet?" Silver sounded far too amused. "You had a candy cabinet? I can't imagine you stealing from it; you're too upright for that."

"Oh, I was a right terror," Ferrin said, and Silver snorted. "Let's get ready, then. I expect it's going to be a long day."

Unfortunately, the morning went by far too quickly. He would have wanted to linger there, watching Silver get ready, pulling him aside to fuck him against the mirror with his breath fogging the glass, but they both had work to do. Not that it stopped Ferrin from *telling* Silver that when he leaned in to swipe the comb from his numb fingers.

"You're sure you aren't a sadist?" Silver asked, and Ferrin just smiled.

Even the walk to the palace went by too fast. Before he could properly register that he and Silver were walking in step, with Silver just in place where Ferrin had told him to the night before, they were already at the palace, and Ferrin was being presented with a summons from the king.

"Yikes," Silver said, and Ferrin rather agreed. He left Silver there, forcing himself not to look over his shoulder like a mooning teenager, and took the side stairwell to King Emile's chambers.

"You do know I have my own plans," Emile said, throwing

open his door before Ferrin could even bring himself to knock. "Come in. Sit down. Have tea."

"I can explain," Ferrin said slowly. Emile pretending at politeness meant one of two things; that he was furious or deeply amused. He prayed for the latter.

"Yes, I'd hope so. Don't mind Bazyli; he's recovering."

Ferrin stepped into the king's bedroom to find Emile's submissive lying on the bed, surrounded by a cloud of little white flowers. He raised a hand in greeting, and Ferrin spotted a line of bite marks on his skin.

Perhaps one day soon, he would leave his own marks on Silver for people to see if Silver didn't mind it. The thought made his dominance stir, and he made himself focus on the task at hand, sitting stiffly on a couch in front of a haphazard tea service.

"You see, my son wanted to be the one to remove Marcel from power." Emile threw himself onto the other chair. "Something about corruption in the guard. Which I'm sure there is—my mother's reign saw to that. I would have done it, but there was the matter of the coronation."

Ferrin frowned, unsure how to translate.

"He means he wants everyone to remember Adrien as a good king," Bazyli said, waving his hand in the air. "Gods forbid they think well of Emile."

"I have a reputation to uphold," Emile said. "And now you're ruining it, Ferrin. A duel? Really? Over the royal tailor?"

"Marcel knows about the crown," Ferrin said before Emile could follow that line of thought. He wasn't certain how to feel about Emile letting matters of state slide so that his son could take credit. Emile loved his son—that was evident—but it felt a bit like trying to play a game with someone who kept flipping the board over. "Tonight, at the duel, the people who informed him or who collaborated with him may come to see how it ends.

I know de Valois is taking over the investigation, but I would like a number of my guards in plain clothes to watch the crowd. And I would need your permission to hold anyone we deem suspicious for questioning."

"See, that's the kind of tactic you'll have to be wary of with my son." Emile took a sip of his tea. "Happily, I don't care. Do what you will. Just don't die. I would rather not lose you so soon before my son is crowned."

Ferrin shifted ever so slightly, but of course, Emile noticed. "Your majesty. I thought perhaps you might be disappointed, given my recent... missteps."

"You've saved my life over a dozen times, Ferrin. More, if you count any internal debates on whether you should simply run me through." Emile's light tone didn't quite match his eyes, and Ferrin wondered how often he suspected that an ally was only waiting for their chance to strike. It seemed like a terrible way to live. He was doing better, of course, since he took Baz as a submissive, but some habits were hard to break.

"So only over a dozen, then," Ferrin said. Emile's smile was knifelike.

"Well. Would it ruin your plans if I attended? I would like to see this, personally."

"Sir, your majesty, it would be a logistical nightmare."

Emile sighed. "I'll observe from a window, then. If Adrien isn't doing so already." He grimaced at the teacup. "There's a spot on this."

"Your fault," Baz murmured from the bed. "You made me prepare it."

"Off the bed, my hawk." It was remarkable how Emile could sound cruel and fond all at once. It was also a clear sign that Ferrin needed to leave before Emile and Bazyli started a scene. He stood, leaving his untouched tea behind.

"I'll be sure not to die, your majesty," he said.

"Good. And best of luck with the royal tailor," Emile added, still watching Baz as he slithered off the bed to his knees. "He seems like a handful."

Not so much, Ferrin didn't say. Silver was, in a way, the opposite of a handful. He wanted rules, thrived on them, and Ferrin had to stop himself from turning down the hall to check on his office when he left Emile's rooms.

Instead, he steeled himself, ignored the stares of passing servants, and made his way to the barracks to brief his guards.

* * *

Silver was—well. It was an odd feeling to be so sated, so *happy*, smiling like a fool and yet sort of vaguely terrified and worried all at once.

It would be just his luck to finally be put under, put on his knees, and then...have Ferrin run through by some odious palace official who barely deserved his title, wouldn't it?

Wait. *Would* it? If his luck were that bad, he'd never have left Diabolos. He would never have survived as a thief in the Guild, and he absolutely wouldn't have walked into the palace and accidentally gotten a job, much less become the *royal tailor*. So maybe he didn't need to worry about it. Maybe Ferrin would be just fine? Unless it meant his luck was all out, and—

"Ah, Master Crowe, there you are."

Silver, who was on his way to his workshop, paused as he recognized the crisp, no-nonsense voice of Isiodore de Mortain. He plastered a smile on his face and turned, greeting the duke with a nod.

Isiodore used to make him very flustered, and it had nothing to do with his title or the fact he was married to the prince. It was that Isiodore's dominance was so strong and less...chaotic, for lack of a better word, than the king's. And therefore, it usually affected Silver much more strongly, though today, he wasn't quite as susceptible. Except if he thought about it too long, he'd think about how Ferrin teased him this morning, putting images of being fucked up against a mirror in his mind, and how could he do *work* when he had to look at mirrors all the time?

Still, Isiodore was a powerful man, and more than that, he always looked both like he knew all your secrets and was utterly unimpressed with them. He was perfectly attired in morning gray, hair tied back with a shiny white silk ribbon, beard neatly trimmed, shoes polished, buttons gleaming. He wasn't wearing gloves, and Silver could see the wedding ring on his left hand and on his right, his signet ring. It showed the insignia of House de Mortain; a raven perched upon two crossed swords. Very fitting, since de Mortain reminded Silver of a raven—which was a smarter, sexier, more mysterious version of the crow he'd taken for his own name. He was very glad he hadn't decided on Raven. That would just be embarrassing all around, wouldn't it?

"Your Grace," Silver said and bowed slightly. "May I be of some assistance?" He felt silly saying it—Isiodore *lived here*; how was Silver supposed to help him in a hallway in his own home?

"Our appointment," Isiodore said smoothly, and Silver blinked at him like an owl as he frantically tried to recall what the appointment might be *for*. Isiodore had allowed Silver to make him a few things for the coronation—mostly to match Adrien's ensemble—but he had his own tailor, and besides, he only ever accompanied Adrien for Adrien's appointments. He'd never made one for himself, and besides, Silver already had the measurements for everything.

But you didn't argue with a duke of de Mortain's status, so he gave a smile and said, "Sure, I was just on my way, sorry. It's, ah, been a long day."

De Mortain pulled out a pocket watch and consulted it. "It's half-past eight."

"Well, yeah, but...long morning," Silver said, but honestly, it hadn't been long enough, or else he'd be pushed up against a mirror, taking Ferrin's cock and being really happy about it. He cleared his throat again, feeling his face flush. "I'm sorry!"

"What for?" De Mortain asked, tilting his head, and then waved a hand. "Never mind. It's a quick appointment, won't take longer than five minutes. Let's be on our way." He had enough dominance in his voice that even though Silver had indulged the night before, it was still effective. Also, he was a duke. And the consort of the future king. Which meant, dominant or not, you did what he said.

Silver made his way to his workshop, and luckily, de Mortain wasn't the type for idle chitchat. Which was fine because it gave Silver the chance to try and think about what this appointment could possibly be *for*. He still had no recollection of anyone making it on the duke's behalf, but he didn't want to say that and get anyone in trouble. The help stuck together, and despite his fancy title, that's really what he was, wasn't he?

"Sorry, it's a little, ah, messy." Silver swung the door open to his workshop, giving de Mortain an apologetic smile. "I've been busy."

De Mortain gave a dismissive wave. "Think nothing of it." He closed the door, then fixed Silver with a sharp glance. "You may stop worrying, Master Crowe. We did not have an appointment scheduled this morning."

Silver blinked. "Uh. Oh. We—didn't?" Good thing he hadn't tried to pretend like he'd remembered all along, then.

"No. I'm only here because, in a matter of, oh, let's see...." Isiodore consulted his pocket watch again. "Two minutes, maybe less, a royal page is going to visit you. He's going to ask that you visit the royal residences, where my husband is going to attempt to convince you to make him and Sabre de Valois some sort of *disguise* so they may attend the duel."

Silver wondered if he should play dumb, but he wasn't very good at that unless he wasn't actually pretending. "The duel."

"Yes. It's absurd, really, imagining the crown prince would attend such a thing. I expected it, of course; Adrien is as bad as his father and still thinks he can move about without attracting attention."

"Oh," Silver said because de Mortain was staring at him expectantly as if waiting for Silver to agree about the theoretical behavior of the crown prince of Staria.

"And I'm sure Emile already attempted to finagle his way into a front-row seat, but I'm assuming Ferrin is smart enough to shut that down," Isiodore continued smoothly. "So I am going to need you to do the same, Silver."

"You want me to...say no to the Crown Prince," Silver said.

"And the Duke de Valois," Isiodore added. "Yes, though. That's exactly it. I should be very cross if you assist them, and no one wants that. Least of all, me. You're Emile's favorite tailor and my husband's."

"Um." Silver cleared his throat. "Thanks?"

"And to make certain, let me make something very clear here, Master Crowe. Captain Marcel is finished here, regardless of what happens today at this duel. I simply won't allow that man to remain near Adrien or Emile, knowing what sort of man he is." Isiodore smiled, cold and sharp. "But I think it would be best if your Ferrin dispatched him honorably—in the duel, of course—and let's make sure that all goes smoothly, shall we? Considering it is, after all, in your honor."

Was Isiodore de Mortain honestly saying he was going to intervene in the outcome of a duel someone was fighting for Silver's honor? "Are you saying—you'll make sure he'll lose, or—"

"No, no. But there are ways I could influence the way this plays out, if necessary. I have faith in Ferrin—he wouldn't still be Emile's guard captain if I did not—and I should like to have faith in *you,* too. Given you are the Master of the *Royal Wardrobe,* I imagine you understand the necessity of keeping the royal family safe?"

"Would they not be safe, watching?" Silver couldn't help but ask, because did Isiodore know something? Were there assassins again, like the one who could change his face?

"I should rather not have the prince of Staria dashing about in disguise to watch duels over matters that could very easily be handled administratively," Isiodore said, with a meaningful look at Silver. "I understand that there are times a person must stand up for something, and while it's appropriate that Ferrin issued a non-lethal challenge, of course, I *could* simply have Marcel brought in and stripped of his captaincy. And I will, if I am required to worry that our future king and his left hand will be dashing about in haphazard disguises to watch."

"I do make very convincing disguises." Silver clearly had a problem; why on earth had he just said that? "I mean. I won't. But I *could.*"

Isiodore gave him a very charming smile that did not reach his stormcloud eyes. "I am certain you could. Another time, perhaps." There was a knock on the door, and Isiodore gave him a polite nod. "Thank you for your attention to this matter, Master Crowe. I believe I shall book an appointment for a new coat. I have had the same tailor for some time, but perhaps a few newer pieces wouldn't go amiss. Adrien does tell me I have a tendency to be, how did he put it...*stuffy.*"

It was hard to imagine anyone saying that to de Mortain, who wasn't stuffy so much as he was...put-together, austere, polished, like steel or silver. He would look dashing in navy, though, perhaps with some satin accents to soften the severity of the design, maybe in white, or even yellow or copper to really throw some contrast in there. "I'll work something up, your grace. And I, ah. Don't think I really have time to make a disguise as good as I would want to for the prince or Duke de Valois."

Isiodore narrowed his eyes. "That isn't the reason I would like to hear, but it shall suffice." The knock came again. "That would be the page, I imagine. I'll let him in on my way out, shall I?"

Silver nodded and idly wondered if it were really de Mortain in charge of the kingdom after all. Probably. He watched Isiodore open the door, and sure enough, a royal page came scurrying in and hastily shoved a message at Silver. "The crown prince formally, um, requests your presents—no, wait, *presence*, in his suites," the page said, looking nervous, looking as new to his position as his uniform, which still had creases from where it had been folded overlong.

His fingers itched to take a steam press to it, but Silver just gave him a reassuring smile and said, "Of course, I'll head that way right now."

The page drew himself up, looking pleased, and bobbed a nod before turning and dashing off. He threw open a door, but it was to the coat closet that Silver kept his own jacket and boots in when he slept in his workroom. The page squeaked, mumbled something, and tried the correct door before disappearing in a blur of new-uniform and anxious new-job jitters.

Silver had to smile. He could remember that being him easily enough, and now look at him. A handsome guard captain fighting a duel over him. The second-highest ranking duke in Staria, issuing vague threats! An appointment with the prince! Life was certainly not dull, was it? And here, his best friend back home in Diabolos, Rowan, had claimed Silver would get bored with city life. Shows what Rowan knew, despite being a witch with three very clever witch moms who raised him.

The royal residences weren't far, and Silver wondered if he would be able to hold firm to his promise to Isiodore as he was ushered into the Crown Prince's drawing room. Adrien de Guillory was charming, kind-hearted, and friendly—and probably learning how to use that to his advantage, likely by the same man who'd just told Silver to tell Adrien *no*.

"Ah, Master Crowe! Is it all right if I call you Silver?" Adrien asked, gesturing toward a chair with a low table in front of it, on which a delectable tea service was already waiting. "Please, help yourself to refreshments. I'm told you prefer sweet over savory, is that right?"

"Y—yes, Your Highness. And Silver is fine. Of course." He sat, feeling a bit at odds about the tea. He hadn't had time for breakfast, what with the start to the morning being a bit chaotic and all, and it did look as if several of his favorites were assembled on the tray; the little cakes with the cream and the sugared oranges, a white-chocolate mousse with intricate nests of spun sugar, even little puff pastries filled with sweet cream. The tea was hot and steaming, a little silver pitcher of milk resting next to the sugar cube dish.

Adrien was smiling at him. He had none of his father's natural dominance, but Silver thought that might be for the best —a dominant with that amount of persuasive charm would be dangerous, maybe, but also, it seemed as if it were just part of Adrien's submissiveness, to be so...welcoming.

This was probably all to butter him up, but Silver decided he might as well avail himself of the tea snacks. "Thank you for the tea." He put some milk and sugar in his cup, stirring it, as Adrien sprawled on the chaise across from him. He looked like the king, though his hair was redder than King Emile's, whose looked almost purple in the sunlight. He was tall like his father but lankier, and while he had Emile's same smile, his eyes were a warm, dark brown instead of icy blue. He also looked vaguely disheveled in the same way as the king often did, though his hair was much neater, and Adrien's particular brand of messy was more cheerful than chaotic.

In comparison, Sabre de Valois looked like a cross between a guard and a noble, which Silver supposed he was, technically. He looked a bit like Adrien and the king—tall, with broad shoulders and a patrician face—but his eyes were a bright, warm copper, and his hair had more gold in the red than either Adrien or his father. He was a quiet man, watchful, who favored simple clothes—the most ornate thing about him was the sword worn at his hip. He was also a submissive, but Silver had always had a bit of a crush on him. There was something so steadfast about Sabre; even if he couldn't put Silver under, Silver still sort of wanted to either climb him like a tree or ask Sabre to stand in front of him as if he *were* a tree. Maybe it was more that, really, than the climbing.

"Your Grace," Silver said, with a nod at Sabre. He was easy to talk to, Sabre, in a way that made you forget he was a noble. "Aren't you having tea?"

"It makes His Highness feel bad if someone is served in his presence," Sabre said and flashed a quick smile when Adrien shot him a glare. It was clear they were close, and Silver thought of Rowan, days spent on the beach collecting shells, climbing trees to get fresh young coconuts, or having dinner at Rowan's with his cheerful horde of meddling mamas. Rowan was also a submissive, but he didn't seem to have a problem with anyone making him food.

"He also ate breakfast before he showed up," Adrien said, with a fond look at his friend. He turned a winning smile on Silver. "So, Silver. You and Ferrin, huh?"

Silver was glad that Adrien at *least* waited for him to take a sip of tea and actually swallow before he said that. He flushed hot, then realized there was really no reason to be embarrassed. He and Ferrin were both adults. There was no reason he should be anything but proud of himself for going to his knees for such a gorgeous dominant.

"Oh, no," Adrien said and laughed. He leaned forward, eyes sparkling, his elbows on his knees. "Sab. He has that look you get, talking about Laurent."

"Or you, thinking about Izzy," said Sabre, and Silver felt completely out of his league as he realized he was taking tea with men who called the terrifyingly competent Duke de Mortain *Izzy*.

Adrien waved a hand. "Yes, yes. Ferrin's a good man. Steadfast, dependable. He's been loyal to my father for years, and I appreciate it. He doesn't always make it easy to do that."

Silver nodded, pretending he didn't see the way Sabre looked away. He and the king had a fraught relationship, that wasn't a secret. Silver also had no idea what to even say to that— he couldn't criticize King *Emile*; he wasn't the crown prince. He was just a tailor who used to be a—

Oh, no. Silver blinked. "He is a good man," he said carefully, glancing at Adrien and then Sabre. "Too good for me, probably?" He didn't mean to make it a question, but he was suddenly convinced that Adrien knew all about his illustrious past as a thief. What if he tried to use that knowledge to get Silver to make him a disguise? Then Silver would disobey Isiodore and go to jail or, worse, end up designing little outfits for noble dogs or something. And Ferrin wouldn't get his victory over Marcel, and then—

"No," Adrien said very quietly. "I think you're a good match, actually. Anyone who can design formalwear that my father will tolerate for longer than an hour should be able to hold their own with Ferrin."

"Oh." Silver sat up straighter. He hated not knowing if his past was being kept in reserve to use as a weapon. He didn't want to get Ferrin in any trouble. "I thought—I don't have the most, ah. Respectable past, Your Highness."

"Adrien," he corrected. And then he smiled. "I once ran off to Mislia on a magic boat, and Sabre used to be a whore. Also, I think being a thief would be interesting." His eyes sparkled. "Do you think you could introduce me to the leader of the Thieves' Guild? I just want to talk."

"Asa," Sabre groaned. "*No.* Izzy'll have my head on a plaque above your bed if you do that."

"I'd make him hang it in the living room, Sab," Adrien said cheerfully while Silver tried to work out if he'd just made his life better or worse, being on a first-name basis with the *future king* —who now knew he was a former thief.

"It wasn't that glamorous, and I couldn't if I wanted to," Silver said quickly. "Part of my oaths I swore when I left."

Sabre sighed, tapping his fingers on the hilt of his sword and giving his cousin a hard stare. "You're just making him more interested."

Of course. It all would sound glamorous to someone who grew up safe, well-fed, and slept in silk sheets. Silver knew that Prince Adrien's life hadn't always been easy, but there were certain realities that you just couldn't escape. Hardships hit differently when you weren't part of the privileged elite. But it seemed Adrien was at least interested in fixing some of the more blatant inequalities inherent in a life made up of nobles and everyone else, and that was something, Silver supposed.

And he really did like his job.

"Well, I believe in second chances, you know. And you're a fine tailor. If the only thing you steal is the heart of my father's guard captain, that's not a problem." Adrien flashed another smile as Silver felt his cheeks go pink. "Honestly, the reason I brought you here is that I want to see this duel, but I know I can't just...go about without some sort of, ah. Disguise."

"Isiodore said he shouldn't, so now he wants to," Sabre translated, arms crossed over his chest. "And where the prince goes, so does his left hand. Even if his left hand wants to smack said prince in the face for this idea."

"Sab, no one is going to pay me a bit of attention," Adrien swore. "Also, I'm curious if this is how people often handle their, ah. Arguments."

Silver ate one last morsel from the tea tray, enjoying the buttery croissant and the slightly bitter chocolate filling as he finished up his tea. "I'm sorry, Prince Adrien. I don't think that I quite have the time today. I have, um. Some things to...finish up." Damn it. He hadn't even thought about what reason to give when he said no.

Adrien sighed and sprawled back on his chaise, looking remarkably like the king when he scowled. "My husband got to you, didn't he? What was it? Threaten to tell the king you were a thief? My father won't care; he likes how you dress Bazyli too much—"

"No, no," Silver said quickly, blushing hotter when he realized he'd just interrupted the prince. First-name basis or no, Silver was still a tailor. "But I wouldn't want to put you in danger, Yo—Adrien. As a former thief turned honest man, we need someone like you on the throne. I couldn't do anything to, um, deprive the country of that."

Adrien and Sabre both stared at him—and then Sabre laughed. It transformed him completely, from a grim-faced man who looked like some ancient warrior, the type they had illustrations of in Diabolos, the ones who used to come from floating fields and fight on wyverback, to a smiling young noble with bright eyes and a warm smile. "I should recommend him for your council, Asa."

Silver winced. "I know how that sounds, but it's true. You don't know how much people here like you, Prince Adrien. People like me—not just former thieves, but the people who work here. You know our names. You're kind. You make people feel like you see them. I know that might sound like flattery, and it is, kinda, because your husband is way more threatening than a man in morning gray with a pocketwatch should ever be—"

"Oh, Izzy." Adrien sighed, chuckling. "He's a terror."

"But it's true. It's also true I promised I wouldn't make you a disguise. I'm sorry."

"You can watch from the window," Sabre assured him, patting him on the shoulder. The light glinted off his signet ring, which showed a stag in a forest, the symbol of House Valois. "Thank you for being responsible, Silver."

"No problem." Silver grinned. "But if I had said yes, I would have made one for you, too, right?"

"Where my idiot prince goes, so do I," Sabre said.

Adrien still looked miffed. "What if I commission a couple of disguises but just for...future use?"

"Well, what you need isn't clothes," Silver said, getting to his feet. "It's a wig. That's how people would recognize you."

Adrien smiled slowly. "An *excellent* point, Silver. I could throw my hair under a cap and wear a hostler's uniform. Don't you have a collection of ill-gotten uniforms at home, Sabre?"

Silver knew they did because he sometimes took commissions from the courtesans in the pleasure district, discreetly, for role-play purposes. Several from the House of Onyx, and even the House of Gold, had contacted him about it. Silver had accepted the commissions before he was made the Master of the Royal Wardrobe and had never *technically* asked if he should stop doing so. The extra money didn't hurt.

"I don't know that you could pull off those shorts of Yves'," Sabre said.

"What? How dare you disparage my ass," Adrien retorted. "Thank you for your time, Silver. I can see I'll have to get up earlier next time to outfox my husband."

He'd probably have to get up earlier than that or never go to sleep at all. But Silver didn't say that. Instead, he thanked the prince for the tea, accepted a handshake, and promised to send along his best wishes to Ferrin—like the duel was some kind of party or a stage play. He really *was* booked for an appointment, so he went straight through the main hall to get to his workshop. There were a lot of people there, mostly nobles on their way to bother the king about something or other, and hardly any of them paid him any attention as Silver politely tried to move past them. He was briefly stuck behind a group of them, though, who were arguing amongst themselves right where the hall met the one that led to the council chambers. Silver had to wait for a moment for them to disperse, and as he did, he noticed a set of pennants hanging on the wall. They weren't new, and Silver had probably walked by them a million times, but he'd never really had the chance to look at them.

There were four of them, in various colors, with symbols etched in various types of thread. A brilliant purple silk shot through with white, gold, and yellow—a sunburst, the crest of House Guillory. Next to it was midnight-blue silk with the outline of a black raven on two crossed silver swords—House Mortain. Next to that was a yellow silk pennant with the stag he'd seen just minutes ago on Sabre de Valois's ring—House Valois's crest. And next to that was a simple white silk pennant with a tree, all dead limbs rendered in stark black. Silver had no idea who that one belonged to, but what drew his eye was the very faint outline next to the white pennant with the tree, as if there was supposed to be another there that'd been removed. He'd have to ask Ferrin. He might not like court politics, but that didn't mean Silver couldn't appreciate a good bit of gossip.

As the group of squabbling nobles finally moved on, Silver headed to meet his first appointment of the day. He had about five minutes to spare before they showed up, and by the time he was ready, charcoal stick and measuring tape in hand, he'd forgotten all about it.

Chapter Eight

The training yards were a menagerie.

Nobles sat on fence posts and jostled each other by the weapon racks, twittering like disgruntled birds. There were a handful of pages clustered in a corner, grinning and passing each other a bag full of fried bread. Guards in plain-clothes—both city and palace, it seemed—milled about anxiously. A group of city guards hadn't even bothered to disguise themselves and were gathered around a preening Marcel, who'd stripped down to reveal a muscled chest that had no reason being that toned on a man like him.

On Ferrin's side of the field, to his surprise, were the palace staff.

"About time someone did this," said Jeanine, the head chambermaid of the royal residences. She was still in uniform, and her wispy hair was sticking up around her cap. She patted Ferrin on the arm. "I've been sending in my own reports on the bastard, same as you, but he just pays the fine and walks off."

"See him walk off from this!" Dione, a scullery maid Ferrin often heard singing in the early morning, grinned at him. "Even the prince is watching, look." She pointed to a pair of men in bad wigs who were sitting on one of the posts. Adrien de Guillory's face was recognizable anywhere—too clean, too polished, a result of a life spent in a place where every blemish had a helpful servant with expensive cream to hide it away. Ferrin sighed and gestured to one of his guards, who started edging close to the prince. That, at least, was one problem he could hide in a safe corner for a while. He was old hat at herding de Guillories by now.

Louise was already at the fence, dressed in trousers and a loose shirt, and she whistled when Ferrin approached. "Look at you, hero of the hour. The way the servants talk, you're their fiercest advocate."

"I'm a piss-poor one, if so." Ferrin settled next to her, scanning the crowd. Silver still wasn't there. "I should have done something other than send useless reports. How many other Marcels are out there, do you think?"

Louise's expression hardened. "Enough. What'll you do about it?"

"I don't know. The guard could handle it, but it seems... there should be a special force for it. People trained not to back down when a noble flashes his privilege."

"And with the power to back them," Louise added. She nodded to Adrien, who was being gently escorted out of the training yards. "You should ask him. I bet he'd do it. Imagine guards who can arrest nobles because a *commoner* charged them to, not just the king?"

"There'd be a revolution," Ferrin said, stretching his arms as Marcel made exaggerated flourishes with his sword.

"That's why you get the king behind you." Louise was watching Marcel, brows knit tight. "You're in a unique position. You should use it."

The trouble was, she was right. Ferrin had spent so long following protocol, utilizing the proper channels, and the most change he'd managed at once was with a slap in the dark and a hissed challenge.

"Hate it when you're right," he said, and Louise smiled.

"Sorry!" Ferrin turned, suppressing a bemused smile, as Silver came wriggling through the crowd. He looked more than a little harried, with his hair a mess and his clothes disheveled from pushing through the throng, and he stared about him as though he expected the duel to already be over. When he saw Ferrin, his face lit up, and the crowd started whispering and jostling each other.

"I thought I'd missed it," he said, staring up at Ferrin. Ferrin smoothed down his hair and adjusted his collar, and glanced to the side to find Dione grinning a little too broadly.

"Something amusing, miss?"

"Oh, no," she said. "It's just nice. My mate Sean always thought Silver here would end up with a pirate, you know. Had five coppers on it."

"People are betting on me?" Silver's brows raised. "Also, no. Ugh. Pirates are foul. They don't bathe, and they kill people for sport."

Someone laughed in the crowd, but when Ferrin turned to look, he just saw the servants pushing closer, forming a protective ring around him. He frowned slightly, and Jeanine coughed.

"Extra measures," she said. "Just in case Marcel wants to send one of his lackeys to stab you in the gut before it starts."

Ferrin paused, momentarily at a loss for words. Louise was right—he would need to speak to Adrien, and soon. "Thank you."

"You're all right, Captain Ferrin," Jeanine said. "Go stab him in the heart for me."

"It ain't to the death, unfortunately," Louise called out, and someone giggled. "But I can challenge him to that if you want."

"Don't get any ideas," Ferrin snapped and turned back to

Silver. He could see the anxiety in the way Silver's gaze kept darting to the crowd, and he stood squarely in his way, drawing his focus. "We're all right, then?"

Silver took a steadying breath. "Yes, sir."

Ferrin hesitated. He wasn't one for public declarations of affection. He always preferred his liaisons to be discreet, if they happened at all. It wasn't a good example, he'd thought, to show an excess of emotion in front of his guards.

He leaned down and kissed Silver, one hand at the back of his neck. "I'll owe you another when I win," he said, and Silver grinned.

"I look forward to it."

"Oh my word," Dione said. "I'll die."

"Calm yourself; look, he's holding his wrist," someone else said, and for once, it was Ferrin's turn to blush. Silver winked at the man who'd spoken, and Ferrin walked him to the fence, which Ferrin stepped over.

"So here's how first blood works," Louise said to Silver while Ferrin took off his uniform jacket.

"I've seen it before," Silver said with a small smile. "I'm from Diabolos, remember?"

"Then you know Marcel might get lucky. That's all he needs. So steady yourself."

"That," Ferrin said, soft enough for only Louise to hear, "was the most unsteadying thing you could have said."

"Then stab him fast and get it over with," Louise whispered back. She whistled sharply when Ferrin started forward. "You're forgetting something. He's your luck, ain't he?"

Ferrin just blinked at her, and Louise winked at Silver. "You ought to know. You're his sweetheart, so you have to kiss his sword before he duels. Give him luck."

"That isn't—" That, somehow, was more intimate than simply kissing Silver in front of the palace staff. But Silver was already hopping over the fence. He glanced at Marcel, who was watching them, and smiled. Ferrin was holding his sword in his right hand, and Silver leaned over to slide his fingers over Ferrin's before bending down to kiss the hilt. When he straightened again, his cheeks were flushed, his freckles dark against pink skin.

"Good luck," he whispered, but his words were cut off as Ferrin kissed him again, harder this time, with none of the soft sweetness of before. This was pure want, coursing through Ferrin like a flame, and when he let go, Silver was breathing hard and smiling weakly.

Ferrin only dimly registered the sound of applause as he cupped Silver's cheek.

"Tonight," he said, "you're going home with me."

"Yes, sir." Silver beamed, and Ferrin turned aside before he lost control and kissed him again. Marcel's face was a stormcloud, and he made a show of shaking out his hands before he took his sword from one of the city guards.

"I challenge you," Ferrin said, loud enough to drown out whatever Marcel was about to say, making him scowl and clench his fist around his sword hilt. "On behalf of Silver Crowe, who you insulted and threatened with physical violence. If you want to end this, I suggest you get on your knees and beg for his mercy."

"Fuck you," Marcel spat. "You whoreson."

"My mother is a respectable woman. Not that whores aren't respectable. On your knees or bleed, Marcel, it's all the same to me."

"Raise your sword, then," Marcel said and lunged for him. The crowd gasped, but Ferrin shifted slightly, letting the sword slide uselessly past him. He kept his own sword lowered.

Marcel snarled and slashed at him—a clever move, with his free arm wrapped around his cloak to cover his open left side—

but Ferrin shifted again, and Marcel overstepped. He stumbled half a step, and Ferrin moved around him like they were dancing under the glittering chandeliers at a palace ball. Someone laughed, and Marcel's cheeks reddened.

"You're trying to make a fool of me," he said, and Ferrin raised an eyebrow. "Stop! Don't you start with that, acting like you're upper-crust when you were born in a gutter, same as that man you're fucking, same as that bitch sister."

"That seems personal," Ferrin said, stepping out of another of Marcel's swings. "You didn't try to proposition her, did you?"

"I wouldn't lower myself," Marcel snarled, but Ferrin could see the lie on his face. Marcel lunged, and Ferrin raised his sword just enough to tap it out of the way. Marcel had decades of expensive lessons to teach him how to parry and riposte, disarm, and slash, but he lacked control. No one told him no, and now he was acting like a child, moving too quickly, lashing out, wearing himself down. He was panting by the time Ferrin rapped on his sword, sending him stumbling back a step. Marcel shook sweat from his eyes, but Ferrin didn't even feel warm.

"I imagine that galled you," Ferrin said. "It would have given you something over me to sleep with my sister. But she knows trash when she sees it."

"I don't need to fuck that bitch to have something over you," Marcel said. "You can't even keep your precious boy's crown safe."

Precious boy? That must have been Adrien, Ferrin supposed. Ferrin pushed Marcel back another step toward the crowd. Marcel's blows were weaker now, and he couldn't hold Ferrin back as he pressed forward. Ferrin braced himself. He had one chance to find out.

"Fool. You think we don't have it back already?"

Marcel's sneer fell, his mouth open in honest surprise. "What?"

"We recovered it last night." Ferrin let his sword slide along Marcel's arm, not quite breaking the skin. "Surely, you know."

"He didn't tell—" Marcel caught himself just in time, but not enough to hide the look of horror creeping over his face. "You bastard."

"Traitor." Ferrin drove forward, forcing Marcel to fight for it, struggling to block Ferrin's blows. Marcel slammed against the fence, and just as he rocked with the impact, Ferrin pierced him through the shoulder.

"Blood!" Louise shouted, and Ferrin grabbed the sword out of Marcel's too-tight grip, flinging it out of reach. He withdrew his blade too quickly, spraying blood over Marcel's shirt, and wrenched Marcel around, so his belly was pressed to the fence post.

"I hereby arrest you for high treason against the crown," Ferrin said, and the crowd erupted into an astonished chorus of voices. Marcel struggled, but he was exhausted and in pain, blood dripping onto the hard-packed sand of the training yards.

Then, Ferrin heard it. A commotion toward the inner door to the palace—someone was trying to run through the crowd, someone in a dark cloak and black gloves. Ferrin, who was dragging Marcel's arms behind his back, shouted to his guards, and one of his people grabbed the man by the back of the cloak.

Just as it seemed they had Marcel's collaborator at last, Hana Lowering stumbled into the guard, knocking him to the ground. The man in the cloak disappeared through the doorway, and the crowd fell into chaos.

"Arrest Miss Lowering," Ferrin ordered, and Hana, her expression blank of all emotion, knelt quietly on the ground with her hands behind her back. She'd expected it, Ferrin realized. She *knew*, and she'd risked her own life to give whoever that man was a chance to run.

"Give me his name, and I'll argue for mercy," Ferrin said in

Marcel's ear, tying Marcel's hands behind his back with his own belt.

"Fuck yourself," Marcel said.

"Then hang on the palace walls," Ferrin whispered. He knew it wasn't likely. The king didn't kill traitors anymore, not since he'd found himself a conscience again. But Ferrin could dream, and he could also feel Marcel trembling, his hands clammy and cool. Ferrin pushed Marcel to the ground and placed a boot on his back to keep him still.

He heard Silver before he saw him, running across the training yards with his boots kicking up dust. Ferrin reached out to steady him as Silver jumped into his arms, and despite the fact that he had a traitor at his feet and a collaborator on the run from his guards, Ferrin laughed. He kissed Silver with his boot on Marcel's back and his heart hammering, and the thrill that ran through him as Silver kissed him back felt like victory.

* * *

Silver was in a daze.

And that was fine, really. The duel ended with Marcel being dragged off for questioning, with Isiodore de Mortain—who was somehow apparently there for the whole thing, despite being without any noticeable disguise—having a conversation with Ferrin in the corner, conducted in low whispers. At the end of it, Ferrin straightened and nodded, then Isiodore said something that made Ferrin cough into his fist and, though Silver couldn't be entirely sure, blush.

He looked over at Silver, though, and the look on his face was full of promise and determination and a million other things that Silver—a brat from Diabolos turned street pickpocket turned thief turned master tailor—felt like he'd stepped into someone else's life, someone else's shoes. How on earth could the beautiful, competent, *amazing* man across the practice yards be looking at *Silver* like that?

But he was, and after Isiodore left to go do whatever shadowy things a Left Hand did when presented with a suspect for a crime no one outside a small circle knew about, he strode over toward Silver like he was marching off to war. He was bleeding dominance so much that Silver was on his knees before he could think about it, unable to help himself, and honestly, why should he even try? It felt so good to kneel and know that his submission was wanted, sought after, that it wasn't just a response to a particular person flinging their dominance about like confetti at a street fair.

Not that there weren't other submissives in the yard kneeling—but Ferrin only had eyes for *him*. And wasn't that sure something?

Ferrin didn't even ask him to stand. He simply reached out and tipped Silver's chin up, smiling just a bit, his dark eyes burning as he stared at Silver. "I have been told I'm to stay in the palace until the king is done with Marcel. De Mortain said *bothering*, but I'm sure he means interrogating, and I've been told to leave this up to King Emile and the duke."

Silver blinked, searched for words, and squeaked, "Oh, okay." Great, brilliant, but he could barely think with the need rushing through him. Being on his knees—even in the position he knew Ferrin liked—wasn't enough. He wanted to get his hands all over Ferrin ten minutes ago.

"I've been given leave to stay wherever I like," Ferrin continued.

"Great," Silver said and then blurted out, "I have no more appointments and my own bedroom in my workshop."

Ferrin smiled and slipped two of his gloved fingers into Silver's mouth. Silver sucked on them, and Ferrin pulled them out slowly, dragging the wet leather across his cheek. It was a gesture of pure dominance, possessive and showy, given they still had a crowd. Which Silver was only tangentially aware of, given how turned on he was, how desperate to do whatever it was Ferrin wanted.

"Then let's go." He frowned, though, when Silver went to crawl—if there was a submissive alive who wouldn't go under watching a handsome dominant duel someone for their honor, Silver wanted to meet them and ask *what the hell is wrong with you?*—and held up his hand. "No. That's not—that's for *me*."

Silver swallowed hard and got to his feet. His cock was so hard, he was sure it was tenting out his pants, but could anyone blame him? "Yes, sir." He saw Ferrin's eyes flash and felt the warm rush of pleasure, the power that every submissive had over dominants who wanted them on their knees, on their backs. When it worked, it didn't feel like giving in or doing something just because of his natural alignment. It felt like sharing some part of himself with someone who wanted it, appreciated it, and was sharing part of themselves with *him*, too.

And all of that pretty much went out the window when they left the practice yards, and people cat-called, clapped, and whistled. Silver's face was bright red, but he was grinning, and Ferrin was holding his hand and half-dragging him back toward the palace like maybe he hadn't noticed the applause and the attendant racket.

"I think they're glad you won," Silver said as they headed into the cool, low-lit palace hallways. He wasn't crawling, but he remembered to keep behind Ferrin, following the protocol Ferrin said he liked. From the flash of heat in Ferrin's dark eyes, he knew it was appreciated.

"I think they're glad I won, too." Ferrin was walking toward Silver's workshop, intent on his destination, and every time someone tried to stop him, he simply nodded at them or lifted a hand to say *not now*.

This was, without a doubt, the most surreal and *best* day of Silver's entire life. Silver was pretty sure the real winner today wasn't Ferrin—it was *him*. And this was only further proven to be true when they finally got into the workshop, and Ferrin grabbed him, shoved him against the closed door, and kissed him breathless.

"This might be my favorite day of my whole life," Silver said, incapable of not sharing this thought with Ferrin.

"I want to fuck you," Ferrin said, staring at him, dominance and lust bleeding from him so strongly that Silver could barely breathe.

"Nope, yeah, it's definitely my favorite day. *Yes*, fuck, please do." Silver dragged in a breath or tried, but Ferrin just kissed him again, and who needed to breathe?

"Can you—how do you want me?" Silver asked, eventually, when Ferrin stepped back enough for him to remember how things like *breathing* and *speaking* worked. "Because look, sir, I really want to do what you want, please, I—I *really* want that." He felt stupid, clumsy, wishing he could just...go make a coat, or something, to show how much he wanted this, to be good for Ferrin, to be *perfect*, for Ferrin to make him perfect. But he'd never been all that good when it came to talking because he was so prone to babbling, unable to be still or think first or do the things suave, hot, sophisticated subs would do for dominants as gorgeous as Ferrin.

Something of his panic must have shown on his face because Ferrin took him by the chin, fingers gentle but firm. "Silver. You're incapable of doing anything else. Take a deep breath."

Silver drew in a long, slow breath. "Sorry. I'm sorry, sir. It's just—do you know that I—since the moment I saw you, I—and I can't, look, I'm better at stuff like—"

"Voice restrictions," Ferrin said, dominance threading

through his deep voice. "But I want you to understand that you are enough. I fought that duel for you, and I'd do it again. You're worth it."

Silver felt his eyes sting, and he nodded, his shoulders relaxing immediately as the pressure of having to speak, to say the right thing, was taken from him.

"There's no way this can go that won't be what I want," Ferrin continued, rubbing his thumb over Silver's bottom lip. "I could fuck you against the door, and it would be enough. I'm not going to this time, but trust me. I would like it. And trust me that I'll make sure you do, too."

Silver drew in a breath, wanting to assure Ferrin that he'd like anything, basically, but remembered he couldn't talk and sucked on Ferrin's thumb instead.

Ferrin gave him a slow, wicked smile. "That's much better. In fact, I know how good you are at sucking on things. Let's go ahead and get me undressed —my boots, first. Put everything away neatly, then come back, kneel, and then you will have earned the right to strip for me."

Silver could do that. It involved clothes. He was good at anything involving clothes, and gods knew he'd stripped Ferrin enough in his mind that this shouldn't be too stressful. With his voice restrictions in place, it was easy to focus on the task at hand since he didn't have to worry about saying the wrong thing. Except he probably couldn't have said anything even if he wasn't on voice restrictions because stripping Ferrin was nothing like he was used to doing at work. His fingers were shaking, but every time he went to apologize, he remembered he couldn't talk, and it was...easier, somehow, to drag in a ragged breath and let himself fumble through the buttons. It was all right. He just had to hang everything up, make it neat, for Ferrin to be pleased with him.

You're enough. You're worth it.

As he worked quickly to accomplish his task, Silver was surprised to find he believed it. He did feel like he'd earned this, the right to submit, to serve, and being quiet with that feeling helped steady his hands. He moved about the room with confidence, hanging up Ferrin's coat, brushing it off, and if he weren't quite as eager to be bent over something and fucked silly, he would have polished up the buttons, too. By the time he'd finished neatly placing Ferrin's boots near the door, he felt...maybe not settled, but secure, and that was a new thing for him. Something about Ferrin's quiet approval and little nods when Silver met his gaze while undressing him was both reassuring and arousing, and he luxuriated in the feeling of it as he worked.

Of course, then he took off Ferrin's pants and underwear and had a good look at him, standing tall and muscular and beautiful, the lamplights picking up the bronze tones in his dark skin, and Silver was on his knees before he even realized it. His shoulders were back, his chin was lifted, and he kept his gaze averted as he waited to pass Ferrin's inspection. Finally, when Ferrin walked over to see how Silver had put his clothes and boots away, Silver *did* get a chance to openly ogle his ass. That was a treat.

"Very well done," Ferrin praised, and warmth rushed through Silver—the kind that wasn't just lust, either. "You may stand."

Silver got to his feet, hands still behind his back, gaze lowered.

"Yes, *very* well done," Ferrin murmured and took Silver by the back of the neck, bare fingers warm on his skin. "Strip for me."

Normally, Silver would feel self-conscious, stripping naked in front of a man like Ferrin. He wasn't tall, or broad, or—beautiful, really, not like Ferrin. But with Ferrin's approval rushing over him like a warm bath, he couldn't find it in himself to be anything but proud.

Silver stripped with far less care than he'd stripped Ferrin, but he knew without being told to go and put his clothes away and do it both quickly *and* neatly. When he returned to stand in front of Ferrin once more, he was naked, eager, and breathing a little too fast...but kept his gaze down until Ferrin gently tipped his chin up.

"That was very good. I want you to suck my cock, and then, I've thought about this often enough—I want you to get yourself ready for me, then ride me. Do you have what you need? You may speak."

Silver flashed a grin at him. "You have what I need," he leered, unable to help himself.

Ferrin rolled his eyes, but there was a smile playing around the edge of his mouth. He patted Silver on the side of the face, not a smack in the slightest, but it still made Silver inhale sharply. Ferrin gave a lock of Silver's hair a tug. "Don't be a brat, or I won't let you come while you're riding my cock. Answer my question."

"I have, ah. Oil. My fingers. A toy or two, maybe a plug, but I...can just use my fingers."

"I want you open, smooth, and slick for me," Ferrin instructed, dominance heavy as he stroked down Silver's throat. "So go and get whatever you need to make that happen. You can see my cock; if you need a toy to get ready to take me, then you'll get one."

Silver just stared at him, brain momentarily fizzing out from lust, and then managed a weak, "Y—yes, sir. It's, ah. In my—my bedroom." He waved a vague hand. "That's over there. The door."

Ferrin looked far smugger than a man standing naked and

hard in the middle of a tailor's workshop should. "Lead the way."

Silver could feel Ferrin's eyes on him as he turned and made his way to his bedroom, only a little concerned at what state he might have left it in—he wasn't a noble, and there wasn't a staff to clean up after him, but as scattered as he could be on occasion in his thoughts and actions, he was a tidy man simply out of habit. It was necessary when you didn't have much space, and while his bedroom here wasn't large by any means, it was the first bedroom he'd ever had all to himself. So he was glad, when he pushed the door open, that the only mess was a jacket slung over a chair and his bed, which he hadn't made.

Ferrin, of course, noticed this. He pointed at the jacket, then raised his eyebrows when Silver made a small, desperate sound of dismay. "The jacket, Silver, and then you'll make the bed."

"But we're just going to mess it up," Silver said, biting his lip to hold back a smile. He wasn't necessarily prone to being a brat, but he liked Ferrin's dominance, and it was too much fun to resist just a little.

"Not if you don't do as I say," Ferrin said, and while Silver didn't think either of them believed that, he went ahead and hung up his jacket and then made the bed in record time.

He found the toy in a chest under the window, grabbed a bottle of oil, and put them on the bed. Then he waited, and Ferrin's smile was bright as he nodded in approval, pulling the chair over and sprawling in it. Silver stared at him, taking in the sight, wanting to be on his knees again just from the way Ferrin looked at him.

"You're so hot," Silver breathed. "Seriously, take that chair with you; it's never gonna look good in here without you in it."

Ferrin laughed. "I was thinking the same about my bed this morning. Speaking of, I'm waiting. On the bed, get yourself ready. I'm going to watch."

Silver's mouth went dry. He managed a yes, sir, and climbed on the bed, reaching for the toy. "How do you want me to do this, sir?"

Ferrin leaned forward, a hand idly playing with his cock, which was so distracting that Silver almost missed what he said. "Lay on your back, start with your fingers, then the toy."

Silver liked his toy, and he liked fingering himself, but he'd never once imagined doing this for an audience before. At first, he wasn't sure he could relax enough to take anything more than two fingers, but it turned out the slight burn of embarrassment at showing off like this really worked for him. He was panting up at the ceiling in minutes, knees bent and legs spread so Ferrin could watch him fuck himself with two, then three, fingers. His cock throbbed against his stomach, already wet, and he bit his lip as he worked his fingers in and out.

"Let me hear you, don't hold back," Ferrin said, and his voice sounded rough, hungry, and Silver could only just see him stroking himself while he watched.

He didn't hold back, and when Ferrin said, "I think you can take that toy now, don't you?" he practically scrambled to grab the toy and get it ready. He dropped it twice, which made Ferrin give a soft laugh. "Eager. That's it. Show me how much you want my cock."

As turned on as he was, there wasn't a shred of embarrassment left when he pressed the tip of the glass phallus against his hole and felt it breach and slide in. He was open enough that it only caused a twinge of discomfort.

"Go slow, that's it. I want to see how it feels going in, every inch, just like you'll take my cock," Ferrin urged.

"Fuck," Silver moaned and pressed it in a little more. He tried to go slow, but it felt so good that he was worried if he went *too* slow, he'd come without a hand on him, and he couldn't do that, *wouldn't* do that. No. He was going to behave, do what he was told, follow Ferrin's orders. "I'm so—fuck, please—"

Ferrin's voice shivered over him, low and full of dominance. "Does it feel good? It looks like it does."

"Yeah, but I—want you—"

"Almost, let me see you fuck yourself, hard, like you want my cock," Ferrin ordered, and Silver had to turn his head and squeeze his eyes shut, count to ten so he didn't come all over his stomach. After he had a bit more control and didn't feel like he was poised on the edge, he started to do as bidden and fucked himself with the slicked-up toy. He started slow, then gradually increased the speed until he was writhing and gasping, sweat stinging his eyes.

"Please, please," Silver begged because he was far too close to the edge to do this for much longer. "Wanna be. Good for you, so good, let me be, please don't let me come—"

"You wouldn't," Ferrin said. "You won't. Keep going."

Silver was half-sobbing with it by the time Ferrin told him to stop. He had to stop twice, and once, he'd tried to bite his own wrist to keep himself from coming, but Ferrin barked out, "No, don't. The only person who will leave a mark on you is me."

Which honestly didn't help that much, the delicious dominance and the flare of possessiveness, but Silver whimpered and fought not to crest that wave of pleasure, though he knew he was at the limit of what he could handle. Ferrin must have known too because that's when he told Silver to put the toy away. And then he felt the bed dip as Ferrin joined him, lying on his back as if he hadn't just driven Silver nearly crazy, smiling over at him with a wicked smile that he should maybe arrest himself for; it was far too attractive to be legal.

Ferrin reached for him and kissed him until whatever breath he'd managed to find was once again nearly gone and pulled him so that Silver was sprawled on top of him. They both moaned, and Silver pushed up, hair in his face, panting down at him. "Want me to suck you?"

"Later," Ferrin said, hands sliding down Silver's chest, pinching his nipples as they settled around his hips. "Ride me, go on. Ask me before you come."

Silver was all out of words, too eager to get Ferrin's cock inside him, and with all the teasing and preparation, he was more than ready. He grabbed the oil, flailing only a little, and was pleased when he heard Ferrin moan as Silver slicked him up. He paused once he was in position, waiting, and Ferrin's head went back as he gasped, "Yes, do it," dominance so strong it felt like a full-body caress as Silver started to slide down onto him.

It wasn't going to last long. At least, Silver knew it wouldn't, for him—unless Ferrin was *evil* and told him no, which was probable and yet didn't stop Silver from riding him hard and fast from the second he was fully seated on Ferrin's cock. It felt so good, better than the toy, better than anything, and he was practically bouncing up and down, making the bed rattle as he found his rhythm.

Ferrin urged him on, hands tight on Silver's hips, helping him move. "That's it, fuck, you feel so good. How does it feel? Tell me how much you like my cock."

"I—love it," Silver managed, the words strangled as he felt his peak start to rise. "So close, sir. Please, please, may I come?"

"Only if you don't touch your cock, you'll come like this, or you won't come at all—"

That was all Silver needed to hear. He threw his head back, crying out as he shifted into the perfect position so that Ferrin's cock rubbed up against that spot inside of him with every motion. He didn't need much more than that, and Silver kept moving, riding Ferrin even when the wave of his own pleasure finally broke, and he came hard, making a mess of them both.

His vision whited out as the pulses ebbed and finally eased, but Ferrin was still hard and hadn't come yet, so Silver didn't stop, even if his rhythm faltered just a bit at the end.

There was a muttered curse, and then the world tilted, and Silver found himself on his back, Ferrin above him, urging him to put his legs around his hips. Silver did, and he could do nothing but hold on and stare hungrily as Ferrin fucked him wildly into the bed, one hand braced on the headboard and the other resting lightly around Silver's throat.

I did this to him, Silver thought hazily, as Ferrin groaned and his face screwed up in an expression of pure pleasure. *I made him feel this good.* He felt himself slipping under as Ferrin dropped his hand, pinning Silver to the bed as he finished inside of him. Silver waited until the last tremor ran through him, then reached up to draw his hands down Ferrin's muscular back, feeling the slick, sweat-dampened skin and luxuriating in how good it felt to be sated and under for a man who more than deserved it. A man who made Silver feel like *he* deserved it, being so...happy, and taken care of, just like he'd always wanted.

I could fall in love with you, Silver thought, feeling Ferrin's breathing even out, his face against Silver's neck. *If I haven't already.* Maybe it would have been a terrifying thought if he hadn't been under...but maybe not. Either way, Silver soothed him with a gentle touch, and then, when Ferrin eventually moved off him and collapsed on his back, Silver turned and flung as many limbs as possible out to attach himself to Ferrin, as close as he could get despite the fact they both needed a bath and the bed probably needed a whole new set of sheets.

"Told you we'd just mess up the bed," Silver mumbled into Ferrin's shoulder. He would be happy never to move again.

"Brat," Ferrin said fondly, and Silver felt as well as heard his chuckle. "But I also don't remember saying we were done."

Silver smiled into his shoulder. That's exactly what he'd

hoped Ferrin would say. "Gimme ten minutes." He lifted his head, took in the sight of a very satisfied and messy Ferrin naked in his bed, and said, "I changed my mind. Five. Five minutes should do it. Maybe less."

Ferrin laughed, drew him close, and kissed him. "You're a delight."

"You're not so bad yourself," Silver said and kissed him back.

Yeah. He could definitely get used to this.

Chapter Nine

The palace was never very quiet at night.

Someone was always awake—whether they were cleaning staff buffing the railings and scrubbing the floors or guards marching through their rote patrols. Tonight, as Ferrin left a thoroughly exhausted Silver asleep on a bed of silks, the palace was full of echoing voices.

He made his way to his office by the barracks, where Isiodore had left a missive in an empty teapot, as expected. He unrolled it, comparing Isiodore and Sabre's notes with the stack of reports left by the guards, and marked where his people were stationed and where the man who fled the duel was last seen. By all accounts, he was still in the palace, which was a chilling thought. Marcel, of course, had said nothing.

Ferrin wrote a note to Jeanine to conduct a discreet search of the servants' quarters, with two of his guards within earshot. It wouldn't do to have guards poking around in servants' rooms. Then he wrote a series of new orders for his guards at the noble residences, who would block the exits. Receiving permission to search the rooms belonging to the nobility was another matter entirely—the nobility had more opinions about the guard poking around than commoners, and they had the power and wealth to make his guards' lives miserable. He wrote the last note for Emile to see when he woke and rang for the few pages who worked the night shift.

They came running, all five of them wide-eyed and far more alert than they had a right to be.

"Did he really wet himself when you killed him?" asked a girl, grinning as she took her message.

"I didn't kill him, and no, he didn't."

She looked disappointed. "Oh. But did he cry?" Ferrin shrugged, and she sighed. "I bet he cried after when he was alone. Everyone says you were *so* handsome."

"Do you have any other messages for us, *Captain?*" another girl asked, glaring at the bloodthirsty page.

"No, you may go." Ferrin tried not to smile as the pages ran off, jostling each other as they pushed through the door. Some of his best guards started out as message-runners. He wondered if he'd see any of their faces in the barracks one day. If they thought it was worth it, being a guard.

He got up, carefully burned his notes, and locked up his office. The message-runners at the bakery were much like the ones in the palace in that way. The thieves' guild picked the best ones and trained them to steal, just as he took in the best pages and set them on a track to one day be officers. Only one group had the promise of a steady income. He wondered if the message-runners in the city had a place to sleep or if they were like Armand and his siblings, barely scraping by, afraid of what ulterior motives lay behind any attempt at charity. It wasn't the sort of thing Ferrin thought about, really—agonizing over every street urchin and stray cat was more Louise's realm, and he was so busy with the palace, besides—but perhaps that was just an excuse. He'd been grateful not to be born into the kind of life where stealing meant survival, and he closed himself off to the people who had no choice. Just like Marcel ignored those he thought beneath him.

He wasn't sure if it was Silver's influence or Prince Adrien's that sent him down this path. But if he wanted Silver, he couldn't avoid it. And oh, he did want Silver. It was ridiculous, impulsive—no one fell for a man within the span of a week or so—but Ferrin had been prone to impulsive things of late.

He'd just locked the door to his office when he heard voices drifting down the hall, growing more urgent by the second. He turned, took a sharp breath, and resisted the urge to sigh as Adrien de Guillory appeared around the corner, flanked by two guards.

"I'll be perfectly safe with two of you," Adrien was saying, which was arguably true, as the guards following him were some of Ferrin's best, but that was beside the point. He had no reason being out so soon after a traitor's co-conspirator was set loose in the palace, and Ferrin strode forward to order him back to his rooms. Adrien spotted him and smiled. "Oh, I know, Captain. I was wondering if I might have a word, and I figured you were either here, or..." he coughed. "Elsewhere."

"Your highness, I'm sure this can wait until *after* certain traitors to the crown have been apprehended."

"Yes, probably, but since I'm here..." Adrien shrugged. "Just a word."

"I hope, your highness, that this isn't indicative of how we'll conduct business during your reign." Ferrin turned to open his office door again and ushered Adrien through, gesturing for the guards to wait outside. Adrien lit the lamp Ferrin had just snuffed, and Ferrin went to his desk, standing there with his hands on his belt. "Your word, Prince Adrien."

"Huh. I *did* catch you at a bad time." Adrien flopped into one of the chairs. "I had questions about Marcel."

"All of which Sabre de Valois and Isiodore de Mortain can answer."

"Not all." Adrien smiled, and for all that he was becoming more and more like his father these days with his casual mannerisms and sharp wit, there was something else there. Ambition, perhaps, but Ferrin wasn't sure that was the right word for it. It reminded him of Louise when she swore she would open her own shop instead of marrying the farriers' boy. "When did this start, with Captain Marcel?"

"When he took his badge, your highness." Ferrin sighed. "He always was a small-minded little bully."

Adrien nodded. "I've recovered some old reports from the staff. Years of reports, apparently, because Marcel was the one in charge of investigating *himself*. But you know, I'm also interested in where it starts with *you*."

Ferrin froze, thinking of old Captain Withers, bleeding out as Emile calmly handed over his gun. "I've never mistreated a servant in the palace, your highness."

"Not that." Adrien tipped his head back, the lamplight casting his eyes in shadow. "I can see you, Captain. Almost like...call it a premonition. You with a new uniform, a new symbol on your badge. A hero of the people. You aren't one yet. No, you're just a man who does his job. But you can be."

"Heroes don't exist, your highness." Ferrin pinched the bridge of his nose. "Knights who rescue fair maidens, noble martyrs—they're just stories we make up to make the world seem better than it is."

Adrien leaned forward into the light. "Yes. And that's what you'll be. People will forget the rest of it, Captain. They'll just remember the good you did. The people you saved. The legacy you left behind. Just like they'll remember my father as a tyrant and my husband as his blade in the shadows. Do you know what happened to Sabre de Valois?"

"What?" Ferrin could barely follow. He wanted to go back to Silver—to leave fanciful thoughts of legacies behind, and return to the hard work of keeping the palace running and idealistic princes dreaming up fantasies. "Yes. He was sent to the House of Onyx. We all know."

Adrien's expression was hard. "Just like I know the names of the nobles who paid to abuse him. Every one of them. It took me some time—Sab was resistant—but... if a person is willing to attack a noble who has already been brought low, what are the odds that they'll treat commoners any better?"

"Low."

"But commoners aren't friends with princes," Adrien said. "Are they? Those people who Marcel harassed, they didn't have powerful friends. But they should."

"Your highness, it's late. We should continue this another time." Ferrin moved for the lamp, and Adrien stood to intercept him.

"Shouldn't they?" His voice was low. "Shouldn't they, Captain?"

Ferrin looked into the eyes of the man who would one day be king. "Yes. Of course, they should."

"Then it starts here." Adrien pulled a folded piece of paper out of his waistcoat pocket and handed it to Ferrin. "With these nobles. This is where it begins for you. Tell me what you need to take them down, and I'll grant it."

"I'll need the law behind me and mine." Ferrin took the paper but gripped Adrien's hand at the same time, holding him there. "Protection from retaliation. The right to act as an extension of the crown because that's all they'll obey in the end. These people, they don't fear a lower-city boy with a badge."

"Then we'll make them," Adrien said. He glanced down, where Ferrin's leftover tea was still sitting, and smiled. "I can see you already, Captain. You're going to be something special."

"I'd rather not speculate." He stopped himself before he could say it, but Adrien was right. Something in him *had* shifted since he challenged Marcel. And the reason for it was currently asleep in bed, yellow hair tousled and his freckles standing out in the moonlight from the window.

"I'm never wrong about people," Adrien said and drew back, slipping free of Ferrin's grip. "You'll figure it out eventually."

He left Ferrin holding a list of nobles, his lamp sputtering in the dark.

It was almost dawn when Ferrin returned to Silver. He had a new list of names rattling in his head now—guards he trusted, ones he'd heard whispering about the nobles and their habits. A few servants who went to him regularly, wanting him to intervene in something outside the palace. They'd need a name, eventually, whatever they'd become, and a uniform. Something to distinguish them from the rest of the guard.

Silver stirred slightly when Ferrin slipped back into bed and curled around him, arms looping Ferrin's waist. He sighed in Ferrin's shoulder, breath warm on his skin.

"Bed's cold," he murmured.

"Sorry. The prince wanted a word."

"I hope it was *goodnight* or *well done*. You smell so nice." He snuggled closer. "So warm. What did he really want, though?"

Ferrin lay there a moment, placing a hand over one of Silver's. "I shouldn't say."

"I'm your man; I won't tell." Ferrin could feel Silver startle, fingers curling. "I mean. Uh."

"Pretty sure we established you're my man when I fought a duel for you," Ferrin said.

He could hear the smile in Silver's voice. "And won. Fought a duel and *won*."

Ferrin rolled over and kissed Silver on the forehead. His cheeks were flushed, visible even in the pre-dawn darkness, but he was still grinning. "This goes no further than us. But you should know."

"Since I'm your man," Silver said.

"Yes. Prince Adrien wants me to...lead a special sect of the guards, I think. People who only answer to him. We would have the power to arrest the nobility if we have to. If a person from the country says a noble is exploiting them, say..."

"You could actually investigate." Silver's smile faded slightly. "That's dangerous."

"So's letting people like Marcel stick around. I think...I might ask Louise if she wants to join. She has her shop, but..."

"Armand's a smart kid. I bet he could figure out how to run the place." Silver laughed. "Do you think she'd say yes?"

"You've seen her."

"True. But you'll need new uniforms." Silver wrapped his arms around Ferrin's waist again. "Something striking. In Adrien's colors, I think, to remind people that you have the power of the crown. And a new symbol for your badge, like a crest the nobles have..."

Ferrin thought of Adrien's voice, dreamlike; *You with a new uniform, a new symbol on your badge. A hero of the people.*

"The nobility love their crests here," Silver was saying. "It'll give you authority."

"I *will* be in danger, though. Even if I'm just in command. Could you handle that?"

Silver looked down a second, then beamed. "Are we making long-term plans?"

"Ah. Well."

Silver kissed him. "I've taken dangerous jobs, myself. And I don't mind. I just have one condition. His highness—his majesty, I guess—has to start giving you time off. And I'm designing your uniform."

"I'm sure that can be arranged," Ferrin said and kissed

Silver back, smiling as the first rays of the sun crept over Duciel, filling Silver's small room with light.

* * *

The knock at the door startled Silver, pulling him out of his half-daydream, half-nap. He hid a hurried yawn in his palm and said brightly, "Come in!" wondering who it could possibly be. As far as he knew, his last appointment left an hour ago. Which he'd mostly paid attention to, given how distracted he'd been all day, and was looking forward to a nice, long hour or so of staring into the middle distance and thinking about Ferrin.

Honestly, how had this even *happened?* He'd somehow made the secret dream of his heart come true, and then some, getting not just a night with a gorgeous dominant but an actual relationship? Silver knew he had Diabolos's own luck, as his friend Rowan always said, and this just proved it. Hell, he felt lucky enough that *he* could steal the crown of Staria if he felt like it. Except he didn't feel like it. Why would anyone want a crown? And it had already been stolen. But other than that, yeah, he felt pretty awesome right now.

The person who came into his office wasn't a noble or one of Silver's other non-noble clients. It was someone he didn't know, dressed in messenger's garb; not a page from the palace, but someone you'd hire off the street. They looked suspiciously at Silver and said, in a gruff voice with the cadence of the lower city, "You the bloke what's called Silver, yeah? Fancy clothes an' all that?"

"That's me," Silver agreed, standing up. He smiled. "Can I help you?"

"This is for you," the messenger said, straightening their shoulders. They cleared their throat. "Um. Sorry. M'new."

158

"It's okay," Silver said, trying for encouraging. "Just, you know. Let me know what it is, yeah?"

The messenger looked at him askance, then cleared their throat again. Silver was just about to offer them some water when they said, all in a rush, "Please come visit the bookstore. I have some news. There's a thing I saw you should know. Okay, thank you!"

"Um, sure," Silver said. He was trying not to laugh. "Who is...who sent the message, though?"

The messenger looked crestfallen. "I forgot!" They hit themselves on the forehead. "I'm so bad at this. I knew I should've taken that job at the laundry. Shirts don't ask *questions*."

"They don't," Silver agreed. "Do you remember, or should I guess?" He had a feeling it was Armand. Louise seemed like she would hire a more experienced runner, but then again, she seemed to have a soft spot for messy people in need of a new situation. "Was his name Armand?"

"Yes!" The messenger sniffled, giving Silver a trembling smile. "That's who it was." They sounded relieved.

Silver gave them some water and a few coins for their trouble, then passed along a cool cloth and kindly showed the messenger to a shaded bench by a fountain outside the palace. They seemed a little overwhelmed.

It was a nice day, and he was whistling a bit as he headed toward Ferrin's sister's bookstore. There were a lot of people out and about, and Silver felt like smiling at every single one of them as he nearly skipped his way to the bookstore. His feet barely hit the cobblestones, he was practically air-walking. Air-skipping.

He stopped and bought himself a sweet milk tea over ice from a stand near the pleasure district, then pushed open the door to Sanctum and glanced around. The bell rang, but other than the sleepy cat, Cuddles, there was no one there. Cuddles blinked her big yellow eyes at him, yawned, and went back to sleep on the stool she was lounging on in a sunbeam.

"Yeah, me too, kitty," Silver said, grinning. He'd like to take a nap, too. With a big, beautiful guard captain—

"Oh, no," a voice said, from the back of the room. "I know that look."

Silver flushed a bit, hands in his pockets as he sheepishly smiled at Louise. She raised her eyebrows. "I mean," he said, feeling about as flustered as the messenger from earlier. Great. He was going to need to sit by a bench near a fountain, too.

"I don't want to hear it," Louise said, but then she smiled at him. "But good for both of you. Armand is in the back. Did the messenger he hired actually make it? I thought they'd pass out the second they heard they had to visit the palace."

"They mostly made it," Silver said and laughed. "I had to guess who sent them, though."

"It's probably a good thing that boy's gonna be a bookseller, not a master thief," Louise said. The bell over the door rang again, and then her voice went sharp, dominance threaded heavy through her words. "No. *No.* I have that sign up for a reason!"

"Ms. Leonhart," a musical voice trilled. "I do apologize—"

Silver blinked as he heard something echo in his head, the loud words of—someone who wasn't there.

WE HAVE RETURNED TO GROVEL APPRO-PRIATELY

MY BOY WILL TELL YOU HOW SORRY HE IS

I AM MODERATELY SORRY

Before Silver could wonder why he was hearing words in his head, a fluffy blue fox appeared out of nowhere...and Cuddles woke up, hissed, and swiped at him.

WHAT

NO

CATS LOVE ME, WHAT IS THIS CREATURE, IS IT ILL

"Flick," said the young man, who had long black hair tied back in a braid with ribbons, and the pitch-black eyes of a Mislian mage. He bowed to Louise. "Ms. Leonhart, I promise he will behave himself—"

"I find one *letter off a pamphlet* missing, Hektor, and I'll send you and that menace back to the House of Onyx with tape over your—"

Silver hid a laugh and ducked into the back room. He knew who the young man was, of course. Hektor Drakos, the actor, whose brother was the king's submissive. Silver saw the small tortoiseshell cat dart through his feet into the backroom, clearly annoyed that a talking fox demon was inhabiting her space.

"You got my message, then," Armand said. He was sitting at a table, copying letters into a workbook. There was a snack in front of him, and Cuddles jumped on the table, flopping down in the way of cats who were displaced and begrudgingly found a new place to sleep.

Silver was glad to see that he was studying, learning his letters—it struck him that he'd never seen that in the thieves' guild. It was good to know that Armand was getting an education, along with his siblings. "I did, yeah. What's up?" Silver sat at the table, chin in his hand.

Armand glanced around, then back at him. He bit his lip. "I remembered something. About, um. The person I saw in the palace."

Silver felt a stir of excitement, but he tried to play it cool. Like Ferrin would, probably. "Oh?"

"Yeah." Armand fiddled with his quill. "I told Louise. She said I should prolly pass it on, yeah? The information. But I don't know if it's helpful. I just...they're happy here. My brother and sister. They really like Louise. And she...we've never had a home before."

Silver thought about being wrapped up in Ferrin's arms, held tight and safe. He knew how that felt. "I don't want to take that from you. I promise."

"Okay. It's not really me," Armand said, defensive, but he wouldn't meet Silver's eyes. "It's mostly for them. You know."

Of course, it was for Armand, too. Here he was, clean and well-fed, absently petting a cat and nibbling on a snack in a warm back room of a bookstore. His clothes were much nicer than the ones he'd been wearing the last time Silver saw him, and he was sure that Louise was providing more than just new boots and a warm, safe place to sleep. A schedule, opportunities, books, a *home* that wasn't dependent on stealing and not getting caught.

"I promise it'll be okay," Silver said, reaching out and patting Armand's hand. "What did you see?"

"The person who...so. I *was* hired to steal something. By a. A bloke in a green cape." Armand fiddled with his sleeve, peeking up at Silver. "I was supposed to get caught, I think. Create a...um. Division."

"Diversion," Silver corrected and nodded. It wasn't an unheard of tactic among street thieves, but the guild prided itself on a bit more subtle approach. "Okay, so you were supposed to be a diversion." That wasn't entirely new information, but after a few moments of chewing on his bottom lip, Armand spoke again.

"Yeah. And he said he'd come get me, right, if I got nabbed. But then Ms. Leonhart did it first, and so. It was okay. But he had a, a fancy ring. With a picture on it. A ring like I ain't ever seen, 'cept on that duke what almost hanged that one time."

"Sabre de Valois?" Silver had no idea where this was going —he couldn't imagine Sabre doing this at all—but he could also tell that Armand was nervous, and he could understand that. It made him think about Ferrin, about the crown prince's burning desire to make things fair. It might never work, but how nice someone wanted to try.

"No, just...I saw he had one of them rings, right, like the bloke what hired me," Armand explained. "And when I was answering questions, the scary one, the one marrying the prince. He had a ring like that, too."

Silver remembered the banners in the hallway, the noble crests, and Sabre de Valois's signet ring. "Was it...a stag?" He couldn't imagine it was Sabre, even given what had happened to him. He was notoriously loyal to Adrien.

"No, it looked like...this." Armand shoved a paper across the table at him. "I don't know, really, but that's what I remember."

Silver looked down at the paper. He wasn't sure what he expected, but the illustration wasn't any of the crests he'd seen on the banner—no stag, no sun, no crossed swords and a raven, no winter tree with barren branches. Instead, it looked like a few sheaves of wheat and...a windmill?

It didn't look familiar to Silver, but he gave Armand another reassuring smile and said, "Is it okay if I show this to Captain Leonhart? I won't get you in trouble, and I promise you and your siblings will be fine here."

Armand nodded. "I asked Ms. Louise first. She said I should tell you. She said it's maybe not right to steal stuff." He looked as if this was a new concept, one he hadn't thought about before.

"Sure," Silver said, though honestly, he might have his own thoughts about what good a crown in a locked case did for anyone. Still, that was true. You shouldn't take what wasn't yours. "It'll be okay. Thanks for this."

Armand went back to his letters, and Silver thanked him and patted Cuddles a few times before heading back out. The actor-mage and his fox were gone, but Silver noticed with a laugh that she was adding *NOT ALLOWED IN STORE, EVER,* to the sign, so he had a feeling that Flick wasn't quite able to help himself. He didn't know how demons worked or how letters tasted, but hopefully the snack had been worth Louise's displeasure.

"How's that man of yours? Fighting duels for you." Louise shook her head, but she was smiling. "I've been waiting for my brother to find someone. Figures he'd do it in the most dramatic way possible. A duel."

"I, um, didn't ask him to do that," Silver protested a little weakly.

She laughed. "But you thought it was attractive, didn't you?"

He gave a helpless little laugh. "It was, yeah. I mean, I didn't want him to get hurt, but I knew Marcel wasn't a threat. And it was nice. Having someone stand up for me."

"That's good. You seem like a nice man. As long as you stay out of trouble, but if you wanted to, oh, make me a new gown, I wouldn't mind." Her eyes sparkled. "Or maybe a suit."

"A suit would—well, excuse the pun, but suit you better," Silver agreed. "Come around once we have all this figured out, and I'll make you one. Something red, bold like you are."

She seemed pleased by that. "Well. All right."

"And thank you, by the way. For taking in Armand, teaching him to read. It's...better for him and the kids."

"Of course it is. Honesty and compassion aren't hard, you know? They're easier than dramatic plans to steal crowns, either the kind you put on your head or the kind in your pocket. If people just realized that, we'd have fewer problems in the world."

Silver couldn't disagree, even if it seemed a bit...easy as an answer. Still, he liked Louise and having her support and acceptance meant a lot. "I'm sort of, um. Maybe in love with your brother."

"Thanks for the most obvious sentence this side of the continent," she laughed. "Go on. Tell Ferrin to bring you over for dinner soon."

Silver promised that he would and then headed back to the palace. He was so intrigued by the paper Armand gave him that he didn't stop to think that maybe he should *knock* on his boyfriend's office door before throwing it open and announcing, "I have a real, bona fide, actual *clue* hot off the presses and...oh, uh. Hi, Your Grace."

Ferrin, who was speaking with the duke de Mortain, gave him a *look*. Gods, he was so fucking hot in his uniform.

"What was that about a clue, Master Crowe?"

"Yes, Silver, do tell us." Ferrin smiled, and he looked like he might want to laugh.

The dominance in the room made Silver want to go to his knees—did Mortain have to just, just be *like* that?—but instead, he focused on Ferrin and nodded. "Yeah. I—someone saw a thing. Here." He pulled the paper out and gave Ferrin a nervous look before handing it over. "I promised the, uh, person who gave this to me they'd be okay."

"Which they will be if you hand it over," de Mortain said.

"I give you my word," Ferrin promised, tall and gallant, and Silver nearly swooned. He handed over the paper. "The person Armand saw in the palace, the day he was, ah, approached to create a diversion with the pearls? He had a crest on his ring. According to Armand, it was the same kind of crest he noticed on yours, Your Grace. Er, not the same motif," Silver amended quickly. "Just the concept."

Ferrin looked at it and frowned. "I thought only Starian duchies had crests, but this one, I don't recognize."

De Mortain took one look at it, swore, and strode to the door and pulled it open, barking for a page. His dominance filtered so strongly through the sharp command that Silver knelt without thinking, then looked up at Ferrin with a slight wince.

"It's fine," Ferrin assured him, reaching down and sliding his fingers through Silver's hair. "I know how they are."

Isiodore was scowling, which wasn't an expression Silver often saw on the unflappable duke de Mortain's angular features, but he leaned against the door and said with a sigh, "My apologies, Silver. It's rare that anything manages to *surprise* me, but that symbol on the paper...let's just say I haven't seen it in quite a while. Ferrin is correct. It's a ducal crest, only...it hasn't been one for quite a few years."

Before Isiodore could explain further, the door was flung open, and the King of Staria came striding in with his son—and a very unimpressed Sabre de Valois—following at his heels.

"Well, what is it?" King Emile demanded, looking as cross as a teenager who'd been told he had to stop doing something fun to see to his chores.

"I found out who tried to steal your crown," Isiodore said. "Or rather, Silver Crowe did."

"No, it was—" Silver stopped as Ferrin gave a sharp tug to his hair and an imperceptible shake of his head.

"Wonderful," Emile said flatly. He crossed his arms over his chest. Behind him, Sabre and Adrien exchanged glances. "Well? Who is the culprit, and I do hope you've apprehended them?"

"Not yet. The culprit arranged for the hapless thief to try and make off with the pearls," Isiodore said, and Silver felt a flare of pity and hoped Armand never heard himself called *hapless*...even if, yeah, okay, that was probably true. "And the thief—"

"His name is Armand, and he's not one, not anymore," Silver said, though it was difficult to make the words come out, given how much dominance was filtering through the room from the king alone.

King Emile spared him a momentary glance, but it was Adrien who said, firmly even without any natural dominance, "Armand, then. And good. I'm glad he found a better situation."

Silver felt a rush of affection for him, this prince who bothered to learn the names of commoners, and cared about what happened to them, even if they were former thieves turned bookshop clerks. Or tailors, for that matter.

"Armand noticed the gentleman who hired him wore a ring, on which was etched a crest," Isiodore continued, staring hard at the king. He shoved the paper at him. "This crest, to be precise. One neither of us has seen for some time."

Silver remembered the banners in the hallway, how it looked like one had been taken down, and things began to make a little more sense.

Emile stared at that paper, and Silver saw the flash of recognition on his face. Adrien glanced over his father's shoulder and said, "But he's—why would—" and then stopped short as the king of Staria drew in a long, deep breath—and then started to laugh.

"Xavier de Sartre," he managed, "you old *dog*."

Chapter Ten

Ferrin was going to take the de Guillorys and lock them in a windowless stone chamber for the rest of their lives.

Oh, he knew that this wasn't technically their fault. Certainly not Adrien's, as he was staring at the paper with abject bewilderment while his father laughed. But it was inevitable, it seemed, that their...their *shenanigans* would continue until the end of time. Besides, he wasn't entirely sure Emile didn't have a hand in this, somehow.

He knew very little of Xavier de Sartre. Nobles ran off or embroiled themselves in scandal all the time. When Xavier made waves in society by snubbing Emile's wedding, his family's expectations, and a good portion of the Starian farmland to run off and play pirate, Ferrin wasn't even a guard. He'd only heard of it because it was the biggest scandal leading up to the royal wedding, and Ferrin wasn't particularly interested in that sort of gossip.

In his time as guard captain, he'd heard of Xavier rarely, if at all. Xavier rescued Adrien and Isiodore in Mislia, but he hadn't stuck around to reunite with the king. Emile had said nothing of him at all when Ferrin delivered the report, and Ferrin had more important things on his mind at the time.

"Your majesty," he said when Emile finally stopped laughing long enough to breathe. "Tell me this isn't an elaborate ruse, and you don't know where the crown is at this very moment."

"Oh, no, I haven't the foggiest." Emile was smiling down at the paper almost fondly. "But he wouldn't settle for anything less than the best. I doubt he's sleeping in a broom closet."

"Would he know Marcel?" Ferrin asked, looking at Isiodore. "Or Hana Lowering?"

"Oh, shit." That was Sabre, who colored brightly when everyone turned to look. "She worked for him. It was before he left, but do you remember, Captain? She worked almost exclusively for dukes—she was in de Sartre's employ decades ago."

"Xavi didn't know Marcel, though." Emile shrugged a shoulder. "He likely saw an easy mark and took advantage of it."

"He knew he couldn't bribe Ferrin, at least," Silver said, and Ferrin ran his fingers through Silver's hair. "But where is he?"

Everyone turned to Emile, this time. His eyes widened. "*I'm* not a spymaster *or* a guard captain."

"But you and Xavier were too alike," Isiodore said. "You knew him best."

"I rather think I didn't at all." Emile's expression darkened slightly. "Considering."

"But if the shoe were on the other foot," Adrien said, "where would *you* be?"

"If it were me, I'd be in my chambers." Emile folded the paper and slipped it into his breast pocket. "I can't imagine staying anywhere else."

"Xavier de Sartre doesn't have ducal chambers in the palace anymore, though," Ferrin said as Isiodore and Sabre glanced at each other. Emile's smile went sharp.

"Of course not. I've been using his suite to store my mother's paintings from her reign. Well, I couldn't very well throw them out," he added when Isiodore choked on something suspiciously like a laugh.

"We should check regardless," Ferrin said, drawing himself up. "Without the royal family in attendance, please."

Emile scoffed. "You are my guard captain, Ferrin. I daresay you can very well guard me."

Yes. Windowless chamber it was.

Emile swanned out of the room before Ferrin could personally tie him to a post somewhere, followed by a sheepish but largely unapologetic Adrien. Ferrin jerked his head slightly at Silver—he deserved to know the truth since he was the one who led them to it—and helped him to his feet.

"Permission to clap him in irons if he's there, your majesty," Ferrin said as he strode ahead of Emile, drawing his sword. Isiodore didn't draw him, but Sabre had a hand on his sword hilt, and Silver kept just behind Ferrin, clearly affected by the dominant energy building in the corridor.

"You most certainly will not," Emile snapped. "Unless it's necessary."

"I would think high treason is necessary, your majesty."

"Oh, you are in a mood. It's that business with the assassin all over again, isn't it?"

Ferrin bit his tongue. He wasn't sure which he preferred—Emile's former paranoia or his current lack of self-preservation. "I can't say, your majesty."

"And I know why," Emile said, sounding far too amused.

When they got to the suite of rooms once kept by Xavier de Sartre, Ferrin half expected the doors to be bolted from the inside. When he intercepted it from Emile, he turned the handle to find the door unlocked, and it swung open easily, revealing a dusty, dim parlor full to bursting with paintings.

Most of them were portraits. All of them were so gauche that Silver, standing beside Ferrin, winced. There were paintings of cats standing on turtles flying through the depths of space, portraits of women dressed as various forest spirits, nude people holding ferrets, and one enormous painting of a half-naked laborer standing in front of a stable, a flower crown in his hair.

"Hello, Father," Emile said.

"Oh, no." Adrien's voice was soft behind Ferrin. "Not really?"

"If you would both stand back," Ferrin said and glanced at Silver. "And you, Silver. It could be dangerous."

Only Silver obeyed.

Ferrin moved carefully between stacks of oil paintings, their frames gilded by the light of the hall. Sabre kept at his side, but when Isiodore made a soft sound between his teeth, Sabre immediately drew back, giving him room. Ferrin gave Isiodore a curious look—he could certainly use that level of obedience from his new recruits—but Isiodore shook his head and nodded to a closed door between two portraits. There was a faint line of light underneath, just enough to be visible from a distance.

Ferrin took the door before Emile could grow impatient enough to push past him and kept his sword drawn, holding himself just out of view. If someone wished to ambush them, it would be devilishly hard to strike Ferrin from that angle, but Ferrin would have a clear chance to run them through.

He pushed open the door, and a warm voice rang out from within.

"Goodness, that did take some time, didn't it?"

Ferrin glanced inside. Xavier de Sartre was an attractive man, with a rakish air that reminded Ferrin a little too much of Emile at his most unsettled. His clothes were immaculate, but he sat on the plush armchair at the end of the room as though he were an unruly child, one leg over the arm of the chair and his lace cuffs dangling. His eyes were hard to make out in the dim light of an oil lamp, but his gaze was sharp, and he had a book resting on the table next to the chair.

"Permission to charge him with high treason," Ferrin said before Xavier could speak again.

"No, thank you." Emile pushed past Ferrin, who growled and sidestepped him, standing between Emile and Xavier. "Captain. If you would move aside."

"Yes, I'm harmless as a kitten," Xavier said. "I take it you're here for the crown."

"And you're the man who stole it." Isiodore's voice was a low rumble. "I may be on Captain Ferrin's side in this, Emile."

Xavier placed a hand over his heart as though wounded, then leaned over and waved. "Your highness. Adrien. Wonderful to see you again. I'd offer you tea, but someone seems to have arrested my maid."

"I'd like an explanation," Ferrin said, and his dominance was heavy enough that he heard Silver drop to his knees at the door. "Now. Damn the tea."

Xavier sighed. "I don't deny that I'm not the most...loyal Starian you're likely to find. I can't exactly receive letters from home anymore. But I've heard rumors, you see."

"Rumors." Emile raised a brow, and Xavier rolled his eyes at him.

"Yes. About you. That you've changed. Gone soft. It used to be that you'd hang teenagers from the palace walls and send poor noblemen off to whorehouses. That was an interesting rumor, I'll tell you."

"Not one you should repeat," Adrien said sharply, and Ferrin glanced at Sabre, whose expression was carefully blank. Xavier looked mildly surprised.

"Very well. But then, all anyone could talk about was how

things were changing. That his highness would be a new sort of king and that the king's weathered heart was renewed by love." He met Emile's gaze, and Emile stared at him levelly, a hand on his hip.

"So you were testing me. How droll."

"Yes, quite. You had three chances." Xavier held up his fingers, counting down. "A common thief—no one would miss him if he were to die. A maid. And a member of your own city government. You could have easily hanged any of them simply by association."

"And if he had?" Ferrin was surprised to hear Silver's voice. He must have crept up while Xavier was talking, but his cheeks were flushed, and his eyes shone. "If they'd hanged?"

"It wouldn't have come to that," Xavier said. "I had plans." But Ferrin thought of what he'd said before. *No one would miss him.* Silver, too, had been a common thief. And Armand had his siblings, who would have starved on the streets or stumbled into danger without him. Hana was a maid with good standing in the palace before this, and now her only source of income was lost, her life in shambles. It was a dangerous, careless gamble as a test, and Ferrin could feel his hackles rising.

"And have I passed, then?" Emile leaned against a painting of a wolf in a bonnet.

"You've surprised me, at least," Xavier said. "Emile. I *would* like a word if you don't—"

"You've had your fun," Ferrin said, stepping forward. "The crown. Now."

"Bossy underlings you have." Xavier smiled and reached under the chair, but Emile raised a hand to stop him.

"Blast the crown. It's just a pile of sticks, Xavi."

Ferrin's fingers clenched around the hilt of his sword, and he turned to face Emile.

"You're wrong." Emile had the gall to look amused, and

Ferrin took a step toward him, ignoring Isiodore's warning look. "No. You'll listen, de Guillory."

"No 'your majesty' anymore, I see," Xavier murmured, but Ferrin didn't even glance his way. He braced himself, standing at attention even as he tossed what remained of his career to the winds.

"Your ancestor was common." Ferrin spat the words, and he heard Silver gasp slightly. "Everyone knows it, de Guillory. When that crown was made, it was supposed to go to the first warrior king who sat on the throne of Staria. But it wasn't a warrior king who took the throne. It was a soldier. A commoner who fell asleep in an empty chair and woke with a crown."

"A fairytale," Emile said, but his bemused expression was gone, and his brows lowered slightly.

"One we needed." Ferrin didn't give speeches. He never roused his guards into fits of loyalty or inspiration. That was Louise's talent. But he could understand her a little more, now, as he stood before Emile. He understood Armand's sullen anger, the world-weary tone that crept into Silver's voice when he spoke of his early life. "Staria can survive without a crown. We can survive without a king. But we keep you around anyway because we know that deep down, you started out as one of us. That you aren't any different than us. That maybe one day you'll stop forgetting us. We made you. That's what that crown is. It isn't the gold one Adrien will wear for the rest of his life. It's just a pile of sticks in a circle like the throne was just a chair, and your ancestor was a commoner. It's a symbol. It means something."

Emile stood there in the breathless silence that followed, blue eyes fixed on Ferrin.

"Being common is the only redeeming quality of the de Guillory line," Ferrin said and sheathed his sword.

Emile held out a hand. "If I may see your gun, Captain."

Ferrin went still. He'd thought this would be how it ended, once or twice, but his fingers shook slightly as he pulled the ceremonial gun from his belt. Emile took it, looking it over, running his fingers over the hammer.

"It pulls slightly when you fire it," Emile said. "Always hits a little left of the heart. Did you notice?"

"I never used it on a person," Ferrin said. Emile smiled, but it was mirthless, his face half in shadow.

"Then you're a better man than I am." He handed it back. "I expect you always have been. If you're thinking of turning in your badge, Ferrin, know that I won't accept your resignation."

"And neither will I." Adrien approached Xavier, his chin tilted. "I'll have that crown now, de Sartre."

Xavier kept his gaze on Ferrin as he reached down and produced the crown from under the chair. It was a tattered thing, made of petrified wood gone rough with age, but Adrien held it gently.

"This is the crown I'll wear as king," he said, looking at Ferrin. "A reminder. And a promise."

Ferrin nodded slightly.

"And I believe we'll have that private word now," Isiodore said, giving Sabre and Adrien a pointed look. "I'll keep his majesty safe, Captain."

Ferrin was glad for the dismissal. He didn't bow to Emile or Adrien. He simply nodded to Silver, who took his arm as he passed and walked briskly through the dark room full of paintings. When he emerged into the hall, he realized he was trembling—with fear, fury, or something else, he couldn't say. His jaw ached, and a headache was building in his temples, but then Silver stepped in front of him and wrapped his arms around Ferrin's neck.

"The king was right," he said. "You're a better man than *all* of them."

Ferrin opened his mouth to object, but Silver kissed him, standing on his tiptoes. Ferrin pulled him in by the waist and lifted him off his feet, and Silver moaned into his mouth.

"So are you," Ferrin said when he finally drew back. "You... made me better. You're making me better. I wouldn't have said that if it weren't for you."

"Yeah." Silver's voice was breathy. "Yeah, I think I love you, too."

* * *

When Adrien de Guillory was crowned King of Staria, it wasn't in the palace.

It happened outside, in the same plaza where his father once hanged traitors to the crown. The flower fields of Staria must have been barren because blossoms carpeted the plaza as Adrien stood there in his cloak and wooden crown, smiling at the crowd. They surged against the line of guards surrounding Adrien, voices rising and falling like the overwhelming crash of the waves at sea.

Ferrin stood at Adrien's right side, dressed in his new blue and silver uniform. There was a symbol of a hawk over his badge now—the name of the new team he would form under Adrien soon—and he could see the nobles eyeing him, whispering, trying to figure out what it could mean. On Adrien's other side, Sabre de Valois held Adrien's ceremonial scepter.

A little ways down, standing with his lover, Emile de Guillory still hadn't stopped smiling.

It was all a whirl for Ferrin. Emile had wanted him to send his best officers to take over the city guard while Marcel wasted away in prison. Hana, whose lover was on Xavier's ship, left with him a few days later, and Armand was probably in the

176

crowd with his siblings and Louise, well-fed and, hopefully, happy.

And there was Silver, standing with the palace staff at the end of the square.

Adrien raised his hand to the crowd, and the city roared.

Perhaps he was right. Perhaps this really was all anyone would remember—that Adrien was loved, that he was a man of the people. That his coronation had, for a brief moment, the slightest spark of magic to it as Duciel seemed to swell to accommodate him. They wouldn't remember a former thief turned tailor or a lower-city boy turned captain. Or if they did, they'd remember them the way they remembered the crown on Adrien's brow. As a symbol of something better.

Adrien turned to Ferrin, and his eyes were bright, his cheeks flushed a faint pink. He raised his voice to be heard over the crowd.

"It's too late to turn back now, Captain," he said and grinned. Then, in front of the city—the kingdom—all the people who would write about this day for centuries to come—he bowed to Ferrin. There was a hush, like a thousand people breathing in, and Adrien straightened. "Lead the way."

Ferrin nodded and turned to the crowd, and King Adrien de Guillory, the descendant of a common man who fell asleep on an abandoned throne, stepped forward to greet his people.

Epilogue

Silver glanced up from the mess on the stove when the door opened, and he plastered a bright smile on his face as he called out, "Welcome home, honey. Dinner's almost ready!"

There was a long pause, and then Ferrin said, carefully, "You...cooked. Again." He came around the corner, still wearing his uniform, a suspicious look on his handsome features. "You know we could always go out. There's that cafe near the swan pond. You liked that one, remember?"

"I did, but I want to make my man dinner." Silver sighed. "But it's...why don't they tell you how long you're supposed to cook things for?"

"They do," Ferrin said, stepping into the kitchen and sliding an arm around his waist. He pulled Silver in and kissed him. "If you read the recipe."

"Recipes are for *quitters*, Ferrin."

"I see." Ferrin smiled, and it was so—so *handsome* that Silver took a minute to remember he had protocol to follow when Ferrin came home.

Silver hurriedly unbuttoned Ferrin's jacket, slid it off his shoulders, then turned and dashed into the foyer to hang it up. "How was your day? And if you hate what I made for dinner, we can go out."

"Finish your tasks, and we'll talk about it," Ferrin said, dominance threaded through his voice, and Silver felt the usual rush as it washed over him. He'd moved in shortly after the coronation—mostly he'd just gone home with Ferrin after the party and never left—but they'd had a nice long conversation about protocol and expectations, and Silver thought it was *Ferrin* who was shy about how much he wanted Silver to follow rules.

Silver didn't mind. He finished hanging up Ferrin's jacket, then went back and knelt there on the kitchen floor to take off his boots. Ferrin made a sound as if he were going to protest, but Silver just beamed up at him and finished with the boots. They'd been over this. Silver *loved* it. It felt so good, being Ferrin's submissive. Almost as good as it felt being beneath him in bed, or on top of him, or standing at his side at important palace functions...

"You're distracted again," Ferrin said and laughed as Silver flushed and shrugged because who wouldn't be distracted, kneeling at Ferrin Leonhart's feet?

He stood up, put the boots in the closet, and then tugged Ferrin down to kiss him properly. "So? How was work? King Adrien keeping you busy?"

"Today, it wasn't King Adrien but our former king." Ferrin shook his head, padding in his socked feet into the kitchen. He sprawled in one of the chairs, and Silver hurried to fix him a drink, which he felt was a much better skill than his culinary efforts. So far, anyway.

"I thought he and Bazyli moved to some country manor?" Silver put the drink in front of Ferrin, who only ever had one, and felt a rush of pleasure as Ferrin sipped it and gave him a pleased nod.

"They're leaving next week. Emile tried to, ah." Ferrin coughed. "He tried to do something. I think I should probably tell you because you might not be...*happy* with me."

"What?" Silver gave a fake gasp. "I'm always happy with you."

"You could have been a consort to a duke."

Silver blinked. "Wait, what? Which duke? You don't mean —not—wait. What?" He couldn't even figure out what this was in regards to or what duke he was talking about. Duke de Mortain was married to *the king,* Sabre de Valois was married to Laurent de Rue, and Duke D'Hiver was a weird recluse who lived in the north and married his musician. Unless Xavier de Sartre was reinstated and so impressed with the court couture, he'd offered marriage to Silver via his...dominant and lover?

"Wait a minute." Silver blinked. "You mean he tried to make you a duke, didn't he." That sounded a lot more logical than offering one's hand in marriage to a tailor based on the cut of the guard captain's coat or the king's submissive's robes.

"He tried to offer me de Sartre's old title." Ferrin sighed. "I said no, of course. The idea of being more involved with the nobility than I actually am? Terrible."

"Yeah, no thanks," Silver said, shuddering at the thought. "Sounds like way too much trouble to me." He had to laugh. "We're probably the only two people who'd ever say that, huh?"

"I'm not so sure about that," Ferrin muttered, but he drew Silver onto his lap and kissed him soundly. "We do have more recruits for the Hawks than I can keep up with already. Adrien's going to be a worse menace than his father."

He probably didn't really mean that. Ferrin liked Adrien, and respected him, which he'd admitted had taken some time with the former king even though he'd come around to it in the end.

"I don't really know what makes people want power and all

that," he said, looping his arms around Ferrin's neck. "I guess if you always go through life feeling safe and whatever, that's just sorta what you think you need."

"Wise words," Ferrin said, kissing his neck. "I did wonder if you'd like it, being a ducal consort instead of a captain's man."

"Nah. First of all, like I trust anyone else to make your clothes? No, thank you. Second, you'd hate it and be miserable, and I like it better when you're happy." Silver smiled at him and then laughed. "I still can't believe I snagged you, somehow. Talk about being in the right place at the right time, yeah?"

Ferrin's firm mouth eased into a smile, the small, private one he only ever gave Silver. "Maybe so. I can tell you what's in the wrong place for too *much* time, though, if you want." He pointedly looked over at the stove, where—

"Oh, no!" Silver jumped up, swore, and immediately grabbed at the handle of a pot that was starting to smell more like the inside of a smithy than dinner. "Uh. Maybe that cafe wouldn't be so bad after all."

Ferrin got to his feet, took up the pot of smoldering charred veggies and pork cutlets that Silver tried cooking, and waved it about a bit. "I'm sure it'd be fine," he said, and if Silver hadn't already fallen stupidly in love with him before, he would have here and now with Ferrin saying a pot full of burned former food was *fine* for them to *eat for dinner.*

"I'm sure it wouldn't be. But let's go out, yeah? I, uh. I can get some cooking lessons, if you want. I like to give you a hot meal when you come home from work." Silver's face heated. "Since I apparently decided I live here, now."

"No," Ferrin murmured, that delicious dominance washing over Silver again. "You didn't. *We* did. I want you here. And if you want to just fix me a drink at the end of a shift, that'd be fine, too."

"Probably better since it wasn't burned," he joked and

nodded. "I can also run out and get dinner if you'd rather stay in."

"It's a nice night," Ferrin said after a moment of consideration. He turned and emptied the pot of would-have-been-stew into the trash, then put it in the sink and filled it with soap. "Let's go celebrate while the smoke clears from the kitchen."

Silver had to laugh. "I'll open a window."

He did and washed his hands—and the pot—while Ferrin changed into something less formal. He still looked amazing, and Silver flushed with happy submissive pride as Ferrin let him do up the buttons on his tunic. He was much better with clothes than cooking.

It was a lovely night, and Silver couldn't really mind the ruined food *too* much. They walked hand-in-hand to the cafe, Ferrin telling him about Adrien's plans to reform the council and include commoners and his appointing Laurent de Rue to oversee the pleasure district. Things were changing in Staria, and Silver was glad to hear that things would get better for the people who didn't have fancy crests on their gold rings or live in a palace where they could look down on everyone else—literally *and* figuratively.

"What happened to de Sartre? Did he and the king—*former* king—ever make up?" Silver asked when they'd been shown to their table outside near the pond because, of course, the person running the establishment knew who Ferrin was and what he'd done. His duel with Marcel was already legendary, and Silver was pretty sure there was a play in the works at Madam Victoria's School for the Arts about the two of them, which was kind of great, really. He'd get to design clothes for someone to play *him*, which would be something, wouldn't it?

"I believe so. I'm told de Mortain was hung over the next day, which I would have never guessed if the prince hadn't told me. The *king*," Ferrin corrected himself. "That's going to take some getting used to. But, yes. I'm told de Sartre left already, but that's probably for the best."

"I don't know. We're pretty good at finding things," Silver said, lifting his wine glass. "Here's to the crown of Staria, which, hopefully, will stay on King Adrien's head where it belongs."

"I'll drink to that," Ferrin said and touched his glass to Silver's. "And I'm glad you don't mind that I'd rather be a guard captain than a duke."

"I'm just fine with it, your grace, as long as *you* don't mind having a former thief around. I can promise I left my stealing days behind me." Silver gave him a salacious wink. "My last great heist was when I stole your heart, yeah?"

He was teasing, mostly, but the smile Ferrin gave him made him feel like maybe it wasn't a joke at all...but the truth.

"Indeed you did, Silver Crowe," Ferrin murmured, voice as warm as the night air, as the rush of affection Silver felt seeing him relaxed and smiling, happy there across the table. "Indeed you did."

In the end, really, that was so much better than a crown.

Bonus Story

Yellow Flowers

Baz wasn't sure what he expected.

He didn't really concern himself much with politics beyond glaring at people who annoyed Emile in a menacing way. So when Emile told him, almost flippantly, that one of his old friends had run off and turned pirate, Baz assumed this was just another quirk of the Starian nobility. Some nobles lived in pleasure houses. Some never appeared at court and were apparently possessed. Others were pirates. That seemed about as plausible as anything else he'd seen at court.

But then the nonsense started with handing down the throne to Adrien, and when trouble inevitably came knocking, it appeared in the form of Xavier de Sartre.

Baz thought Emile might kill him at first. Then, to the bewilderment of everyone except Xavier, Emile just laughed.

Isiodore de Mortain looked about as pleased as a basket of hornets, but Emile pulled up a chair in Xavier's dusty, abandoned suite and poured himself a glass of wine.

Then another.

Then a fifth.

Then, when almost all of de Sartre's wine bottles lay empty, and even Isiodore joined in a rousing chorus of *The Farmer's Cockerel Is Hardy Indeed*, Baz picked Emile off the floor and announced they would be leaving.

"Oh, don't be like that, Bashleigh. We've only just started catching up," Xavier said. He still had yet to get Baz's name right once, which Baz suspected was deliberate. There was some sort of history there between Xavier and Emile, and no matter how friendly they were after several bottles of wine, Baz suspected his presence wasn't entirely welcome.

"I'm quite capable of getting to bed on my own," Emile said as Baz dragged him out the door. "Imagine. Xavier. In my own palace. That bastard."

"Why is it that sounds like a compliment?" Baz asked. Emile gave him an arch look.

"Because it is. I'm a bastard myself. So are you. My son, in fact, is an anomanomly."

"I have no idea what word you're butchering."

"Wouldn't even come to my wedding, can you imagine?" Emile was practically falling into Baz's arms, now. It helped, somewhat, that Baz had once dragged Emile across the city, but he still wasn't very muscular, and they both started tilting dangerously as Baz guided them into Emile's rooms. "I was going to put him in puffed sleeves, and he ran from me."

"Puffed sleeves is a good reason for piracy, I guess." Baz slammed the door shut after them and looked at Emile. "You're too drunk to bathe. Go to bed."

"Don't try to dom me in my own room," Emile said. He tried to tweak Baz's chin, missed, and turned to the bed. Baz pushed him onto it, and Emile glared at him. "That's...you on your knees, then."

"Obviously, because you aren't going to take off your own

boots like this." Baz didn't drink much for this exact reason—he hated not being in control of his faculties, feeling like he was back in the brothels of Mislia with drugged smoke fogging his mind. Emile didn't indulge either, save for when noble pirates happened to be visiting, apparently. But Baz had dealt with him when he was poisoned half to death, and he supposed getting trashed was a similar condition.

"You should show more respect to your dominant," Emile said, lying on his face with one boot off.

"Yes, yes, I respect you. Now stop wiggling so I can take off your pants."

"See, that's what...what I should be saying."

Baz rolled his eyes, tossed Emile's boot in the corner—no one ever said he was a tidy submissive—and shoved the man he loved onto the bed like a slug stuffed in expensive clothes.

"He looks well for a pirate," Emile said as Baz started undoing Emile's clothes. "Don't you think so? All that sun didn't ruin his features. He must have made a deal with a demon."

"It's why Mislians don't age," Baz said automatically, quoting the tired old joke every Mislian heard at least once. "Is he...the sort of man you like?" If he was, Baz couldn't see the appeal. Xavier didn't look particularly attractive, in *his* opinion. Certainly not the kind of man you would get drunk over.

"Why?" Emile looked at Baz too keenly for someone who had that much wine. "Did you find him pretty, my hawk?"

"No. I found him smug, maybe, and...like a noble." Emile raised his brows, and Baz blushed, discarding his own clothes so he could climb into bed. "You know how nobles are. They have an air to them. Like they can get away with anything because they deserve it for having the right parents."

"An assumption which is patently untrue and will be more so when my son takes the throne." Emile smiled as though that pleased him very much. "But Xavi isn't that type of noble."

Xavi. What kind of nickname was Xavi? It was the kind of nickname you gave a...a pompous little lordling who showed up out of the blue with his *Hello, Emile,* and his *I hope you don't mind that I'm sitting here all seductive in my fucking chair with my fucking legs and my open fucking shirt, Emile.* Xavi. If Baz had to call him that, he would go sleep in the garden.

"Well, that's a scowl if ever I saw one." Emile pressed a finger to the middle of Baz's forehead. "Is this the matter of the coronation? It's all resolved now, of course. Naturally. Nothing to worry about."

"But a pirate got into your palace," Baz said, but Emile was already drifting off. Of course. Baz lay there for a minute, listening to Emile's breathing go slow and even, and rolled out of bed. He walked barefoot to the balcony overlooking the garden and swung it open, peering down into the lush flowers and creeping vines.

"Ambrosia," he whispered. "My girl."

The flowers rustled, and he felt his demon—such as she was—enter his mind like a worried mother coming into her son's room to find it a disaster. He could feel her wanting to tidy it up, fussing over his tangle of emotions, and relaxed at the familiar warmth of her presence. He was growing used to her absences, now that she lived in the garden for most of the day, but she'd been his first and oldest friend.

"I don't know what I'm feeling," he whispered. It was probably unfair to rely on a demon to sort out his thoughts. He had to get used to doing it on his own eventually. But there were some times that he needed Ambrosia's perspective, and he smiled as flowers started blooming in his hair. He plucked one and stared at it, squinting a little.

"Yellow hyacinth?" He frowned. "That means jealousy."

He felt Ambrosia's presence flare in his mind, pleased as always that he remembered her lessons. But that wasn't the point. The point was that Baz wasn't...he couldn't be jealous. Xavier was just a pirate who happened to barge in at the wrong time. That had nothing to do with jealousy. He tossed the flower into the garden and scowled when he felt others blooming under his fingers: buttercups, this time.

"I'm not being a *child*," he said, as Ambrosia's disappointment pushed up against his own thoughts. "I'm not. He's just, oh, you know."

It was just that Xavier had known Emile since they were children. He was smart and charming, and he had a ship full of people he could boss around, just as Emile bossed around Isiodore and his nobles. He and Emile were alike enough that anyone would think they were a decent match. While Baz wouldn't even have a glass of wine and had to pull Emile away before they were done catching up.

"Oh, gods," Baz said, putting his head in his hands. "I *am* jealous."

About a dozen flowers sprouted up around him that represented some form of sympathy, and Baz groaned as Ambrosia tried to radiate comfort. He sat down on the balcony, too mortified to return to the bedroom, and covered his burning cheeks with his hands as a cool breeze swept over the hyacinths.

* * *

There was a reason he did not drink.

Emile woke up with a mouth that tasted like the sands of Arktos, a headache that made him think someone was mining for marble in his brain, and a stomach that felt like he'd just dove into a whirlwind at sea. It was altogether unpleasant, as was the faint knowledge that he didn't much remember getting back to bed and was asleep on top of the covers.

It was still dark out, which was...horrifying, considering he used to be able to sleep past dawn after drinking too much wine, even if he couldn't honestly remember the last time he'd done so. For all his faults, Emile was too paranoid to enjoy being drunk and didn't often indulge—maybe with Lianne when they were first married, though his wife could drink anyone under the table without breaking a sweat.

Emile winced and sat up, pressing a hand to his head though it did very little to mitigate the small army marching about inside of it. He glanced around, but his submissive was not curled up asleep at his feet, nor was he lying in bed beside Emile. It was dark enough that he knew it was still hours before dawn, and Bazyli wasn't much of an early riser, so he doubted Baz was up and about already.

He swung his feet over the bed, giving a slight groan as his stomach rolled, and his equilibrium took a second to catch up with the movement. Wine was terrible. Why hadn't he remembered that? Emile took a deep breath and got to his feet, and there was enough light in the room that he could see his clothing had been tossed haphazardly in the corner, along with his boots. He smiled. "Bazyli?"

Even the sound of his own voice, quiet as it was, made his head hurt. Honestly, what had he been thinking? He'd been poisoned at his son's wedding. Wasn't that enough to swear off drinking? Apparently not. Emile grabbed a dressing gown and pulled it on, steadying himself for a moment as he looked about for his submissive. Bazyli wasn't anywhere to be found, but there was a pot of tea on the low table near the window. It was on a warmer, and there was a sprig of fresh mint in the teacup, which meant Bazyli was somewhere nearby as he'd made the tea.

Emile poured himself a cup and drank it almost without stopping, heedless of the temperature being just a bit too hot for it. He drank the second one slower, scanning the suite, and it wasn't until he turned around that he saw Baz.

He was asleep on the balcony, long-limbed and lovely, curled up on a bed of moss.

Emile sipped his tea, taking the time to let it ease the worst of his headache—and the churn of his stomach—as he beheld Baz there, asleep on the terrace. His face in the spill of moonlight looked almost too lovely to be real, with his long, dark hair and those sharp, angular cheekbones, skin pale as snow, as graceful as a statue.

There were flowers all around him, and Emile smiled, finishing his tea and placing the cup back on the table. He opened the door and went out into the cool night air, the scent of flowers a comfort instead of a torment.

"Well, I'm glad you didn't let him wander too far, Lady Ambrosia," Emile said and felt a tickle of a blossom behind his ear and the faint, earthy taste of clover in his mouth. He made a face—it wasn't the clover Baz made him eat when he was poisoned, but it was hardly *appetizing*. Still, it did help somewhat, and he nodded his thanks to Baz's lady as he quietly pulled the door open and went outside.

The fresh air was also good for his head, and he went on his haunches and gently placed a hand on Baz's shoulder, shaking him. "Baz? My hawk, why are you sleeping on the porch?"

Baz blinked his eyes open. They were dark blue and sleepy, and he had a suspicious look on his face that made Emile want to kiss him. After he brushed his teeth, probably.

"I didn't mean to fall asleep," Baz said, voice husky. "Are you alive, then?"

"If I'm not, then what befell *you*?" Emile asked, running his fingers through Baz's hair. "Yes. Suffering my poor choices, of course, but that's part of drinking too much wine with old friends, I suppose."

"Old friends," Baz said flatly. "He stole from you."

"Yes, well." Emile shrugged. "He'll be gone soon enough. Or else I'll keep him here, make him work his family's wheat farm. He won't last a week." Emile sat on the porch because the fresh air was doing more for his middle-of-the-night hangover than anything. "I take it you didn't care for him?"

"He's very...." Baz wouldn't meet his eyes. "Smirky."

Emile's eyebrows raised. "Yes. He's infuriating; he always has been. He brought my son, Isiodore, and your brother here, though. You know that, yes?"

Baz blinked. "Oh. Hektor doesn't...he doesn't talk much about that, the journey."

Emile knew why—Hektor had been brought to Staria silenced, with his demon fox, Flick, locked away in his mind. "So, you see, he's done me a favor. Returning my son and my left hand and bringing your brother."

"You didn't even want Hektor here," Baz said, and the waspish tone of his voice made Emile's brows raise again.

"Yes, but then you followed along, and while I would have preferred you not be sent here to kill someone, of course, I am quite pleased how it all ended up," Emile reminded him.

"Are you?"

Emile stared at him. "Bazyli. We're *married.*"

"Yes." Baz sighed.

"Don't sound so happy about it." Emile frowned. "Why *are* you sleeping on the porch?" There was a proliferation of yellow flowers, with the sort of intensity that made it feel like a punctuation mark. "Your lady is trying to say something."

"No, she isn't," Baz said, which was, of course, wildly untrue.

Emile studied him. Baz wouldn't meet his eyes, and he looked—guilty, of all things. "Did you poison him? Is that it?

Something I should know about before he turns up dead in his family's unused suite?"

"What?" Baz startled. "You're not serious. I'm no killer. Is that what you think of me?"

"No, but it's the middle of the night, and I must confess, Bazyli, I have no notion *why* you're out here or what you're—" he stopped. A thought occurred which was so ridiculous that he almost laughed. "You're not *jealous*, are you?"

The flowers again. Emile did laugh, then. "Bazyli. Xavi and I have known each other since we were in diapers."

"You were lovers once," Bazyli said, and Emile could hardly believe it. He was *right*.

"Yes, we were. We're both dominants and—dare I borrow your phrase—*smirky*. How do you think that went?"

"Well enough that you're still mad he did not attend your wedding," Bazyli said. He made a face. "I am not proud of this, Emile."

His expression was so severe that Emile leaned in and kissed him. "Bazyli. If there were feelings there, they weren't on my end. I have only ever loved two people in my life. One is dead, and one is you, so I should think you have no reason to be jealous of a man I was not convinced shouldn't be arrested."

"Well, you do like complicated people," Baz huffed. "And you love your son. Isiodore."

"Of course, but you know what I mean. Bazyli, I can assure you that my only feelings about Xavi are a mild amusement that he became a pirate, lingering annoyance that he left me to fill his role on the council with *Lord Chastain* of all people—so you can see how well that worked out—and hope that when he leaves, he doesn't take any more priceless artifacts with him."

"Hmm," Bazyli said. He sighed, then leaned in and put his head on Emile's shoulder. "It is absurd of me. I know this. That's why I came here, outside. I have...never been jealous before."

"No? Well, how flattering." Emile reached and took his hand, giving it a quick squeeze. "As lovely as the fresh air is, I'd like to go back to bed. Quite rude of my advanced age to spring the hangover on me in the middle of the night instead of the morning, as it should." He got to his feet, pulling Baz up with him.

"Do not drink so much wine," his submissive said because, of course, he did.

Emile pulled him in and kissed him again. "You have no reason to be jealous, Bazyli. It was nice to see Xavi again, but I'm no more interested in going to bed with him now than I was when he left. I...think perhaps I was a bit harsh with his feelings when we were younger."

"You? Never." Bazyli smiled a bit. "You don't need to do this. Reassure me. I was being foolish."

"Yes, well. You're my submissive, and if you need reassurance, you'll have it." Emile left the doors to the patio open as he tugged Bazyli back toward the bed. "I'd show you exactly how you're the focus of all my attention if I wasn't sweating wine, so perhaps you'll allow me to demonstrate in the morning."

"Oh, I suppose." Bazyli freed his hand, then went to the tea. "You should have more. You'll feel better in the morning."

Emile groaned and flopped back on the bed, less like a king and more like someone with a hangover who'd stayed up drinking too late with old friends. "If you say so."

"I do. And, hmm. You must be poorly if you're so agreeable to being topped from the bottom."

Emile could just make out the curve of Bazyli's smile as he ducked his head to prepare more tea. "Oh, you'll pay for it tomorrow, I assure you. Now, bring me that tea and perhaps massage my temples. Show me what a good submissive you are, attending to my needs even if they're a result of my own foolishness."

Bazyli shook his head, but he laughed as he brought Emile the tea and curled up on the bed beside him, catlike and sly. "Drink all of it," he bossed. "I don't want to have to flog myself in the morning."

Emile shook his head and drank his tea. It did help, and when he put the empty cup on the bedside table, he felt much better. Enough to sleep, not to wield a flogger or fuck his gorgeous submissive, but that could wait until the morning.

As he climbed under the covers, he felt Baz move to slide down and sleep at his feet—he must be feeling out of sorts; he usually only did that when he was under—and Emile made a soft noise. "No, up here with me."

Baz complied, but he was tense, stiff-muscled as Emile wrapped himself around him. He bit gently at Baz's neck, smiling against his skin. "I'm not displeased you were jealous, you know."

"Yes, that's why I didn't want to tell you," Baz said.

Emile laughed. "I imagine so. If you like, I'll tell Xavi that I'm terribly sorry, but the king's submissive has decided he should not be allowed on Starian shores—"

"You don't have to pass a *law*," Baz huffed, but there was a smile in there somewhere. "I am sorry if I was terrible, Emile. I am...not used to this. Being in love. It comes with, ah. A lot of emotions I am not used to."

"Yes, well, I forgot most of them, so we're quite the pair, Bazyli." Emile yawned. "Now, let us go to sleep. Thank you for the tea. In the morning, I imagine I'll be quite up to the task of making you the sole focus of my affection *and* my attention."

Baz scoffed, but Emile felt him shiver a little and smiled. He closed his eyes, felt himself start to drift off, and thought what a strange thing it was to have someone jealous over him. Not the crown—no, he was used to that with as many attempts on his life as there'd been—but *him*, Emile, who soon would be another noble in a court that no longer had to do as he said. Adrien would be the king, and Emile would drag Baz off to some country estate and finally lay down the burden of holding the kingdom for Adrien. Adrien would be a good king, and Emile could find out what sort of man he was without the crown.

Perhaps with a little less wine, too.

* * *

"Apparently," Xavier de Sartre said, leaning on Emile's doorframe, "I have broken seventeen laws, one of which is *making a fucking nuisance of yourself.* Thank you for the reminder, Izzy."

"Any time." Isiodore stood a little ways behind him, looking like he hadn't had a single glass of wine in his *life.*

"Which means I have to leave before I corrupt your court," Xavier finished. He glanced past Emile, who was standing in the door only half dressed and beautiful, and looked at Bazyli. "But I feel as though you've been thoroughly corrupted without me."

Baz, who'd been blissfully under for the past fifteen minutes and saw no reason to drag himself out, slipped on one of Emile's robes. It was one of the expensive ones, not silk but soft and richly embroidered, and Baz had taken most of them when Emile ignored them all for plain, basic colors or nothing at all. He tied the robe tight—didn't want Xavier seeing the marks on his ass today, thank you—and walked over to kneel at Emile's side, effectively blocking the door.

Yes, Emile had proved well enough that Baz didn't have any reason to be jealous, but he found that his mind wasn't always reasonable, and he privately wanted to bare his teeth at Xavier like a disgruntled cat. Emile pulled at Baz's hair, and Baz smiled faintly.

"He's hardly a corrupting influence," Emile said, stroking

Baz's hair and tugging it again, keeping him trapped in that blissful, quiet state. Xavier gave Baz a searching look, then turned to Emile again.

"I don't know about that. You would have had me hanging on the walls a few years ago. When I heard you'd taken a Mislian lover, I thought he was more of a war prize. We have a Mislian on my ship," he added to Baz. "My first mate. Her demon's a cat who lives in her hair. I suppose you don't have one."

"She's in the garden," Emile and Baz said at once, and Baz smiled faintly, leaning against Emile's legs. Xavier's brows rose.

"They can do that?" Xavier shrugged. "I simply mean that, well. When you're bored puttering around the palace listening to your son make the kind of mistakes early rulers always do, you might allow a corrupting influence to appear at whatever disgusting country estate you retire in. Now and then, you know. When I don't have a crew to pay."

Emile glanced at Baz, probably looking for a hint of the jealousy that coiled traitorously in his chest. "Of course. We'll take you on horse trails to see the nearby farms."

"Fuck, I knew there was a reason I left." Xavier's smile faded slightly, and he looked down. "You know. About that. It wasn't my family as much as it was...me being young and foolish. Could've gone about it a different way, perhaps. Stayed for the wedding."

"Is that an apology?" Isiodore asked, and Xavier glared at him.

"He'd eat nails rather than apologize," Emile said. "And you're forgiven, of course. But you really should stay for the coronation. So long as you don't give my son the coronation gift you intended for me."

Isiodore paled. "You don't mean the goats."

"It's traditional," Xavier said, crossing his arms. "The first king of Staria was given four goats and a bushel of wheat. So it has historic precedent, and no, I didn't sneak goats into your palace. That would mean I'd have goats on my ship. I keep my quarters clean, thank you."

"Whatever poor submissive you've ensnared must be a practical butler," Emile said, and Xavier shrugged.

"They don't last long. And neither should I. That cousin of mine isn't coming to the coronation, is he? The quiet one, d'Hiver? He was always *looking* at me when he was a boy."

"He's sending his...housekeeper," Isiodore said. "Apparently. And his ward."

"You do keep a strange court, Emile." Xavier flashed another one of his too-charming smiles. "I'll stay, but only until the dust settles. I have a crew to return to, after all. But you'll..." He looked down at Bazyli and away. "You'll be all right."

"I still don't trust you about those goats," Isiodore said and took Xavier by the shoulder. "We're searching your rooms again."

Emile watched them go, a bemused smile on his face as Xavier and Isiodore bickered, and Baz wondered what they must have been like as young men. Whether Emile had been tempered by love, yet, or was still all rough edges and bristling thorns. He preferred the man he had, in any case. Bristles and all. Emile glanced down at him and tugged his hair lightly, making Baz gasp.

"There you go," Emile said. "He likes you. That was, in his way, as glowing an endorsement as he could ever make."

"But he didn't even say my name."

"He wouldn't." Emile drew Baz back into the room and leaned down to kiss him. "He thinks you made me a better person."

"I just stuffed you full of clover and scowled at you," Baz said, and Emile looked, if anything, more pleased than before.

"Well, you'll have plenty of scowling to do today," Emile said, sauntering over to the closet. "We have to formally promote Adrien in the council this morning, which means a brunch with my nobles, who will try to fawn all over him in hopes he doesn't have them up on charges of, oh, commoner mistreatment or something. It'll be delightful."

"It sounds terrible."

"Mm, yes, which is why you'll be wearing...the tassels, I think. It'll make you look properly menacing," he added, smiling over his shoulder at Baz.

"As menacing as a butterfly," Baz grumbled and went to join him. Emile wrapped an arm around his waist and kissed him again, surrounded by expensive, colorful clothes Emile would never wear.

"I can't wait to torment you in the countryside when this is done," he said, and Baz laughed.

"Neither can I."

Coming Soon

STORM FRONT, the first book in Iris Foxglove's new *Immortals Descending* series, is out this October! This series follows five immortal beings — embodying the concepts of Death, Desire, Dreams, Disaster and War — as they find their eternal mortal companions. This series is set in the same world as the previous two, and will feature several familiar faces — and places — from earlier books.

In a remote village, a man named Azaiah goes wreathed in flowers and smiling to the sacrificial altar, willing to die to keep his village safe from plague. But the Harvester has something else in store for Azaiah, and it isn't the shores of the world beyond that await him...but the cloak and scythe itself. Being Death means a long life that nevertheless requires a connection to humanity, and Azaiah learns that corruption awaits those who do not find a mortal companion to keep them tethered to the world. He finds it in Nyx, a soldier from an ancient empire and an adopted son of the Emperor, whose soul burns bright enough that Azaiah is certain immortality won't be a burden but a gift.

But then a shocking betrayal changes Nyx from a gruff soldier with a kind heart to a man bent on vengeance, swearing fealty not to Azaiah, but his sibling, Ares. With Nyx set on destroying the empire that was once his home, Azaiah is dangerously close to losing himself to the corruption that threatens those who lose their tether to the mortal world.

Nyx once loved the Empire and the family that took him in, but when the perfidy of his adopted brother results in a tragedy beyond his ability to bear, Nyx wants nothing more than to burn the world in his wake. Turning from the quiet, intriguing Azaiah toward the promise of bloody vengeance, Nyx gives his vows to Ares and watches the empire he once served fall into ruin. But as the years pass, vengeance is a cold comfort, and the man who is now called Glaive is determined to save Azaiah from being lost in the dark.

COMING OCTOBER 10, 2022

Pre-Order your copy today!

Also by Iris Foxglove

THE STARIAN CYCLE

The Traitor's Mercy

The Duke's Demon

The Prince's Vow

The Exile's Gift

The King's Mage

A STARIAN TALE

The Last Flight of Marius Chastain

SEASONS OF THE LUKOI

Winter of the Owl

Spring of the Wolf

Summer of the Wanderer

Autumn of the Witch

IMMORTALS DESCENDING

Stormfront (October 10, 2022)

About the Author

Iris Foxglove is a shared pen name between two longtime fantasy readers, Avon Gale and Fae Loxley, who are committed to writing fun, escapist queer fantasy featuring decadent, kinky stories, intricate worldbuilding and unforgettable characters.

Loved the book and want to help indie authors produce more unique content to enjoy? Leave a review on Amazon, Goodreads or wherever you like to review books. Don't forget to tell a friend!

Connect with Iris:

If you're interested in receiving information on new releases, sign up for Iris' newsletter!

If you're interested in monthly bonus content, exclusive excerpts and other perks, consider becoming a Patreon! Monthly content is available at just $1 a month!

Iris also has a Facebook group if you'd like to check it out: Iris Foxglove's Poisoned Garden